## "I think this will look lovely with your gown."

Luke took a box from his coat pocket and pulled out a delicate wrist corsage with a single small gardenia.

"Thank you, Luke," Eugenia whispered, moved by his thoughtful gesture.

She wanted to laugh and joke and ask him if he did this for all the contest winners, but if he did, she didn't want to hear about it. She sensed that this was going to be the most splendid night of her life; she didn't want even a negative thought to spoil it.

"Are you ready, my cohost?" Luke asked after he had put the corsage on her wrist.

In the ballroom beyond, the band had already started to play fifties music. Eugenia told herself that she could die and go to heaven at this very moment without ever having missed a thing on earth. She felt beautiful. Luke was by her side. And the moment was pure glory.

Dear Reader,

Welcome to Silhouette—experience the magic of the wonderful world where two people fall in love. Meet heroines that will make you cheer for their happiness, and heroes (be they the boy next door or a handsome, mysterious stranger) who will win your heart. Silhouette Romance reflects the magic of love—sweeping you away with books that will make you laugh and cry, heartwarming, poignant stories that will move you time and time again.

In the coming months we're publishing romances by many of your all-time favorites, such as Diana Palmer, Brittany Young, Sondra Stanford and Annette Broadrick. Your response to these authors and our other Silhouette Romance authors has served as a touchstone for us, and we're pleased to bring you more books with Silhouette's distinctive medley of charm, wit and—above all—*romance*.

I hope you enjoy this book and the many stories to come. Experience the magic!

Sincerely,

Tara Hughes
Senior Editor
Silhouette Books

# BRENDA TRENT

# Be My Baby

*Silhouette* *Romance*

Published by Silhouette Books New York

**America's Publisher of Contemporary Romance**

Everyone we meet, whether only a passing acquaintance or someone who becomes a lifetime friend, affects our lives in some way. As a longtime writer, I'm still surprised and gratified by both complete strangers and old friends who are willing to share.

Tara, thanks so much for helping me enrich *Be My Baby*. Dave H., super disc jockey, thanks for the time and info. Loder, thanks a thousand times. Jean, thanks (but still *no* French silk pie!). Pat, Katy and Michael, June, Lois, Sue, Eileen, Alice and Bill, I love you! (And, yes, a special thank you to Bobby, Sarah, and Janet.)

SILHOUETTE BOOKS
300 E. 42nd St., New York, N.Y. 10017

Copyright © 1989 by Brenda Himrod

ISBN: 0-373-08667-9

First Silhouette Books printing August 1989

Silhouette Romance

Silhouette Special Edition

Silhouette Desire

---

# *BRENDA TRENT,*

the author of numerous novels and short stories, is an inveterate traveler who has visited most of the U.S. and much of the world, but confesses that the home in Virginia she shares with her husband and pets is her favorite place. Her firm credo is that life is to be lived and love is what makes it viable. Her passions include reading, movies, plays and concerts. But writing, she says, is her biggest passion and truly what makes all the rest of life meaningful.

# —Remember—

when your mother used to shine your Mary Janes with Vaseline?

when your crinolines were starched stiff enough to stand alone?

when drive-in movies and milkshakes, hot dogs and popcorn were a special date?

when you could stay in the soda shop for hours sharing a single Cherry Coke with two straws?

when you could phone your favorite disc jockey and request a bebop love song while you and your sweetheart listened at a drive-in restaurant?

when dance partners actually held hands even when the music was fast?

when couples really believed in moonlight kisses and vine-covered cottages for two . . . with baby making three?

# Chapter One

Eugenia Latrop tightened the clasp in her straight, pale blond hair as she entered the kitchen where her sister sat at a small, round table.

A song from the seventies was playing on the oldies radio station, and she listened for a moment as Lindsey sang along with a famous female singer. Then Eugenia adjusted her glasses and through the sliding glass door that led to the beach, she gazed out at the rolling swells of the ocean.

The song ended and the disc jockey's voice boomed into the room. "Good morning, beauties. Luke Newton here. I hope the day is looking good to you. I know *you*'re looking good. Glad to have you join me."

"I'd be delighted to join you," Lindsey said aloud. When she looked up and saw Eugenia, she giggled. "I love that man's voice," she said, pretending to shiver at the thought of him. "I'll bet he could whisper sweet nothings to a woman all night."

Before Eugenia could comment, Lindsey motioned to a chair. "Come on and sit down. The coffee's hot and the rolls are delectable."

"It's so marvelous here," Eugenia said as she joined Lindsey. She smiled as her blue eyes met those of her younger sister. "You live such a glamorous, exciting life, Lindsey. Look at what you've accomplished," she said, gesturing to the pretty wicker furniture that added to the casual atmosphere of the charming beach house. "You're only twenty-three. I'm so proud of you."

Lindsey grinned. "Oh, pooh, Genia, you sound as if I'm ages younger than you are. You're only twenty-five. I was earning bucks while you were increasing your brainpower in school. I was lucky to be in real estate and get a good deal on this house when it came on the market, but other than the house, what do I have that you don't? Heavens!" she said, her voice exaggerated with mock despair. "I'm beginning to think we're both going to die old maids!"

Eugenia laughed delightedly. "Now you're the one sounding as though you're ages older than you are. You still have plenty of time for marriage."

"To whom?" Lindsey asked dryly, then popped the last bite of a doughnut into her mouth.

Smiling, Eugenia said, "Your problem is you scare all the men away, Lin. You certainly meet plenty who're interested, but they want to do the chasing. You're so bold and free with your thoughts and ambitions."

"This is the eighties, for heaven's sake!" Lindsey retorted. "A woman can do her own thing these days, and men shouldn't be intimidated."

"It may be the eighties," Eugenia said, "but statistics indicate that men are more intimidated than ever. They still want to do the courting."

"Well," her sister responded, "if we're going to be blunt and honest this morning, I have to say that I don't see that your way worked any better than mine, big sister. You went with old what's-his-name for seven years. Seven years! And *then* he married someone else."

Eugenia looked back at the water. "It was all for the best," she said. "Daniel and I weren't right for each other, or it would have worked out. We would have eventually gotten married."

"Pooh!" Lindsey cried. "He wanted someone more 'with it' than you, Genia. You've got to loosen up, girl! Get rid of that old-fashioned image of yours. I swear I think Mother cursed you when she named you Eugenia after Granny. You're out of step with the times, lady. If you had forgiven Daniel his 'little indiscretion,' he still wanted to marry you, but you were so uptight when you found out he was seeing that other woman."

Eugenia's words were carefully measured. "I considered that a blessing, Lin. If a man cheats before marriage, how on earth do you think he'll behave after the vows are taken?"

Lindsey waved a hand in a careless gesture. "He's a man, for heaven's sake! Not a piece of clay, Genia. He couldn't wait for you forever. I mean, first it was finish high school, then it was finish college, then it was get your teaching career under way. Of course he found someone else in the meantime."

Several someone elses, Eugenia thought to herself, but she didn't want to recall the shock she'd felt when she learned about Daniel's "little indiscretions." She didn't want to remember any of that. It was in the past, anyway.

"I didn't want to marry him after I found out," Eugenia said simply. "Obviously he didn't really love me, and we just weren't meant to be married."

In truth, neither she nor Daniel had been in any hurry to marry. She'd felt no uncontrolled urge to spend her nights wrapped in his embrace, and he certainly hadn't pressed her to set a wedding date. Sometimes she wondered if she wasn't as relieved as he that the relationship had ended. She was very much afraid that he'd become a comfortable habit, and that both of them had worried too much about what their family and friends would say, if they called off the wedding after being a couple for so long.

"How can you say that so casually?" Lindsey practically exploded. "I know you cared that he had another woman."

Eugenia nodded, trying not to focus on her shattered pride. "Of course I cared, but I got over it. I learned a good lesson, too. He really wasn't for me, Lindsey."

"After you wasted seven years?" Lindsey cried, then bit into another doughnut.

Shaking her head, Eugenia murmured, "I didn't consider them wasted. I thought I loved Daniel. We shared many good times."

"And some not so good times," Lindsey reminded her. "You fought a lot."

That was true, but Eugenia had no intention of going into that with her sister. She and Daniel had different values, she had discovered. It hadn't been as easy to put him and the seven years behind her as she indicated to her sister. Finally she had succeeded and she honestly believed it had all happened for the best.

She and Daniel had even remained friends after the breakup, at least on the surface, but maybe she had only done that to save her pride. She really wasn't sure.

Still, she believed in marriage and living happily ever after with one man who would love only her. If that was old-fashioned and naive, so be it. It was her philosophy, all the same, and somewhere someone else believed it, too. She had to trust in that.

She smiled. "Good heavens, Lindsey, when I complimented you on your cosmopolitan ways, I had no idea how liberal you were. I might be old-fashioned, but I believe in fidelity. If men like Daniel are fine with you, then I'm afraid you and I have a different outlook on marriage."

Lindsey's face reddened a little. "To tell the truth," she said pensively, "I don't think I could put up with infidelity, either. The worst thing for you must have been finding out that he'd had another woman all along and other people knew, but you didn't. I know how worried you are about your image as an 'educator.'"

It was a joke the two sisters had shared since they were teenagers. Eugenia had announced at the dinner table one night that she'd decided to be an educator, finding the term much more dignified than plain old "teacher." Everyone had laughed, including their parents. But Lindsey's announcement that she intended to take the easy way and marry a rich man had elicited even more laughter.

Eugenia smiled at the memory. "I do worry about my image, it's true, but thank God, I outgrew that pretentious stage." She laughed. "You obviously haven't outgrown looking for a rich man."

"Nope," Lindsey agreed. "You've achieved your ambition, and I'm ever pursuing mine. You know what

Grandmother said: It's as easy to love a rich man as it is to love a poor one.''

Eugenia laughed. "Grandmother, my eye! Lin, Grandmother never said any such thing. In fact, she said that real love is all that matters. She said it would see a couple through rich or poor times. You altered that bit of advice until it's pure Lindsey."

Lindsey hooted with laughter. "You know I never was good with words, just with 'm and m's'—men and money, and not necessarily in that order. By the way, Brad and I are going dancing tonight. Let me have him fix you up with a friend of his. The guy's a looker, and he's got money."

"Oh, Lin," Eugenia said with a sigh, "I don't think so. Frankly, I think *you*'d stand a much better chance of finding true love and marriage if you stopped searching so hard."

Lindsey laughed. "Come on, Genia, you've got to get out and go for the gold, as they say, or you'll be left still standing on the train track when all the cars are loaded."

Eugenia chuckled. "Lindsey, if you're trying to shock me, it's too late. I think your philosophy is closer to the truth than even you realize. Look beneath the surface of those wealthy, handsome men you date and see how shallow they are. They aren't looking for marriage."

Lindsey laughed again. "*They* may not be, but I'll sneak up on one and get him in spite of himself," she said, her fingers creeping across the table toward the doughnut box to yet another chocolate-covered goody. "Attack and capture!" she cried, grabbing up the sticky confection and biting into it.

Unable to keep from laughing, Eugenia could only shake her head. "I hope it works, although I have my doubts," she said.

"Well, what about tonight?" Lindsey repeated. "Let me get you a date."

"No, thank you, really," Eugenia said. "I'm not ready for the social scene yet. I don't like the idea of a blind date."

"I think that's another outdated term, Genia," Lindsey said with a chuckle. "I think we just refer to strangers as new men now. However, speaking of blind, I might tell Brad to bring someone who wears thick glasses though, unless I can convince you to put on something of mine. You *dress* like a schoolteacher!"

Eugenia took her sister's teasing good-naturedly. "I'm perfectly comfortable in my own clothes, thank you. Haven't you heard, anyway, that miniskirts weren't such a big hit the second time around? They're quickly fading from the fashion scene."

"That may be, but I'm wearing mine to the last, bitter day," Lindsey insisted. "And it wouldn't hurt you to try one."

"Now I say pooh!" Eugenia declared. "Me in a mini! Ridiculous! You, Lin, have always been the sexy one, the fashionable one, though only God knows how you keep that figure, the way you eat sweets constantly," she noted, assessing her five-foot-four sister's curvaceous figure.

Lindsey giggled. "Jealousy, oh, jealousy!" she said teasingly, knowing her sister watched her weight. Then she sobered a little.

"Seriously, Eugenia, you're a good-looking woman. If you'd only do a little something more with yourself... I have an idea," she said, snapping her fingers. "Let's put some highlighter on your hair. And I'll tell you something else. If you'd eat an extra doughnut or two, you might put some curves on that willowy, five-foot-eight frame of yours.''

Smiling, Eugenia shook her head. "I'm as naturally slender as you are curvey, Lin. You know that. I'm satisfied with myself."

"You know, that's another problem of yours," Lindsey said, wagging a chocolate-coated finger at her sister. "I honestly believe you *are* satisfied with your life. My word, woman, who could be satisfied with teaching first-graders and volunteering at nursing homes? *Boring!* And I do mean boring!"

"To each his own," Eugenia said. "I love my life."

"Pooh! You're like an old lady," Lindsey insisted. "All that education muddled your brain, messed up your priorities. You were born fifty years too late. Your view of the world is fogged over. Anyway, if you don't find a man, how are you going to have all those babies you want?"

For the first time, Eugenia sighed. She did want children desperately, and for that she *would* require a husband, despite the trend toward single parenthood. Oh, she knew she was out of step with the eighties. Maybe Lindsey was right; maybe she had been cursed by Granny's name and was hopelessly old-fashioned, but she knew what she wanted in life. She would settle for no less.

She had achieved a lot of her dreams; she did love teaching and she loved the elderly. She derived great pleasure from simple things. In fact, her most valued possessions in her apartment were the pictures the children had drawn especially for her, and a crocheted bedspread one of the ladies at the nursing home had worked on for two years, just for her.

Sure, it was true that Daniel had shaken her up and made her realize how badly she could be hurt, but she'd finally worked it all out for herself. And she did believe she would have all of her dreams one day. She was that idealistic—or that foolish—depending upon who was judging her goals.

Reaching across the table, Lindsey squeezed her sister's hand. "I'm being a little rough on you, big sister, but I really do know what's best in this case," she said conspiratorially. "You need a new man in your life. That's really what you have to do—replace the old one with a new one. It's time you started dating again."

Eugenia smiled fondly at her sister. "I love you, Lin, and I know you love me and that you mean well. It's just that I'm not ready yet," she murmured. She wanted to change the subject. "I really do appreciate your inviting me here to spend some time with you. I needed to get away."

"I know," Lindsey said softly. "I knew that the moment Mom called to tell me that Daniel's wedding announcement was in the paper."

Eugenia met her sister's eyes again, seeing the compassion and the concern. "I meant I needed to get away from my routine," she said quickly. "Lin, I wasn't widowed, for heaven's sake. The man just decided he wanted someone else, and I decided I needed a vacation. School has been out for weeks, thank goodness!"

Unconsciously she folded her hands in a prayerful pose and rolled her eyes upward. "The mothers are getting the pleasure of three months with their little darlings."

Lindsey laughed. "You enjoy teaching and you know it. You probably wish there was no summer break."

Eugenia laughed, too, the sound soft and golden like her hair. "Now you're really off track. Yes, I love teaching, but I need a breather from all those sweet little mouths calling my name a hundred times a day."

"Pooh! You can't wait to have a dozen of your own," Lindsey declared.

"Those will be calling *me* Mommy," Eugenia said, "and anyway I only want four, preferably two girls and two boys. I'll take whatever God gives me, of course, and just pray that they're healthy."

"Huh," Lindsey said. "He's not going to give you any until you find a man. Now come on. Agree to go out with Brad's friend."

"No," Eugenia said, finally losing her patience. Good heavens, Lindsey was more persistent than a seven-year-old!

"Daniel's getting on with his life, and you must too, Eugenia," the younger woman said firmly.

Eugenia reached for the coffeepot and poured herself a cup. "Mmm, that smells good," she said. "And these rolls look fatteningly delicious."

The smooth, sexy voice of the disc jockey on the radio intruded again, filling the room with the husky sound. "Good morning to you pretty ladies who are just arising, and you, too, gentlemen," he said, his voice naturally deep and low, and as rich as dark chocolate. "Luke Newton here."

"Doesn't he sound absolutely delicious?" Lindsey murmured dreamily.

Eugenia smiled at her sister. "I'm afraid I don't share your enthusiasm for the man. I think he sounds incredibly arrogant. I wonder if he has cause to see himself as such a prize."

"Today's the day, people!" Luke Newton boomed unexpectedly, his voice sounding big and exciting. "You men don't need to listen to this if you don't want to, but you know what day it is, don't you? I'm about to announce the lucky winning woman! Yes, indeed, I'm going to make some lady's day today!''

"Listen to him, Lindsey," Eugenia said, shaking her head. "Make some lady's day, indeed! He's probably as big as his voice." She made a barrel shape with her arms.

"Shh," Lindsey whispered. "I want to hear him."

"Don't tell me you entered the contest!" Eugenia cried. She had listened to Luke Newton, every morning since she arrived in Myrtle Beach last week. She wouldn't want the man as a prize, no matter what came with him, no matter what he looked like.

Sitting very still, Lindsey chewed anxiously on her lower lip as she waited while Luke stretched out the game, teasing and talking, his voice becoming deeper and deeper as he drawled the names of several women in a sexy, Southern accent.

"And Suzie Nelson—is not the winner," he said. "Nor is Darcy Ashley. The winner will be the third name I draw. Sorry to disappoint you, ladies, but maybe another time. We have a contest, and I give myself away every single year."

"I'm sure he does it more often than that," Eugenia declared, her voice low.

Lindsey didn't say anything. Looking as if she were glued to her chair, she listened intently. Eugenia studied her sister's face and was unable to miss how excited Lindsey was.

"You did enter, didn't you?" Eugenia asked. "Why on earth would you want to win a contest with Luke Newton as part of the prize? What's the story on him, anyway? I seriously doubt that he's rich. He hardly sounds like your type."

"Shh!" Lindsey hissed.

"And now, ladies—ladies, get ready!" Luke teased, still dragging out the announcement. "The moment we've been waiting for all these weeks is at hand! Right now some lucky lady is going to shout and holler. She's going to not only win a three-day vacation right here in Myrtle Beach at a fantastic, brand-new resort hotel as my cohost for our Fabulous Fifties Fun Frolic, she's going to be treated like royalty. All kinds of extras are included: a beauty make-over, free clothes, fabulous dinners, a fifties Cadillac at her disposal. Even photo sessions, and who knows where that might lead? It's going to be grand, I promise, and would I lie to you?"

"Is he for real?" Eugenia asked in exasperation. "Talk about a man with a monumental ego problem!"

"Now don't get so excited that you forget the number," Luke said, repeating it for the third time. "You have to call me within ten minutes. Then I'll verify your identity, and, fortunate female, you're going to be queen for a weekend!"

Lindsey clasped her fingers together and leaned toward the telephone as she repeated the number to herself.

"The winner is—" Luke played the suspense to the hilt. "The winner of the Fabulous Fifties Fun Frolic as honored guest and cohost with me, Luke Newton, compliments of your favorite station is—"

Lindsey looked at her sister and chewed her lip again. Eugenia shook her head.

"The winner, ladies and gentlemen, is *Eugenia Latrop*! Call me, Eugenia, you lucky gal, and let's make plans," Luke said, lowering his voice. "Come on and call. I want you by my side for the party of a lifetime."

"You won!" Lindsey squealed. "You won, Eugenia!"

Eugenia refastened the clasp in her hair and frowned. "I didn't even enter. There must be two Eugenia Latrops in South Carolina, and better her than me. I'm not interested, trust me."

"*I* entered you, and you won!" Lindsey cried. "Hurry up and call. Ten minutes go by quickly."

"*You* entered me!" Eugenia repeated incredulously. She looked at her younger sister. "Well, you should have entered yourself. I'm not going around the block with that man, much less to a resort hotel as his guest and co-host for three days!"

"Don't be ridiculous!" Lindsey cried. "Hurry up and call before he draws another name."

"No!" Eugenia said firmly. "I'm serious, Lindsey. You should have entered yourself. I don't like the sound of the man or the party! I'm not hostess material, at any rate. That's up your alley, not mine. No way. Forget it!"

Lindsey sighed in exasperation. "I entered us both, Genia. Fate determined the winner. Now stop being foolish and call, for heaven's sake."

Eugenia shook her head firmly. "No way. I'm not interested. Let him draw another name." She snapped her fingers as a better idea occurred to her. "You call and say you're me, Lindsey. You want to do it, and he won't know the difference. Say you're Eugenia Lindsey Latrop."

"You're being foolish," Lindsey said in disbelief. "This is a dream contest. Luke is a dream man. It's destiny. This is a way for you to get back in the social circle and get a new lease on life. Good heavens—a complete beauty make-over, clothes, photo sessions. The list goes on forever."

The list made Eugenia shudder. "Listen, Lindsey—"

"No, you listen, Eugenia. It'll be fabulous! It really will. A fifties weekend! What fun! I've always loved those old fifties movies, and so have you. The dances and the costumes. Ponytails and poodle skirts. The bunny hop, the stroll. Dick Clark and American Bandstand reruns. The simplicity and innocence of the decade. You know all the old songs—'baby, baby, baby,' 'bebop, bebop,' 'rock-rock-rock,' and 'sha la la.' Come on, a step back in time is right up *your* alley!"

Almost ecstatic, Lindsey approached the phone. "Now hurry up, for heaven's sake, before he *does* pick someone else."

As though to reinforce her sister's words, Luke came back onto the air, his voice urgent and coaxing. "Only seven more minutes, Eugenia. Come on and call before you lose out."

"Before *I* lose out," she muttered. She shook her head a third time. "You go, Lindsey, or let him pick someone else. I don't want to sound ungrateful, and I know you entered me with the best of intentions, but I'm not going to do it. Thanks, but no thanks."

"Eugenia—"

"No! I'm not about to go back in time for a nostalgic, gimmicky hotel promotion with a stranger for the weekend. And that's exactly what it is, you know. It's a radio-hotel promotion."

"So what?" Lindsey cried. "It's legitimate and wonderful and you won! Call! Hurry up! You just can't say no, Eugenia! You claim to be a romantic! Well, think about this—dancing cheek to cheek, listening to dreamy music about love and romance, dressing up in old clothes for the occasion."

Eugenia obstinately shook her head. She couldn't even conceive of agreeing to such a thing. "You can't be serious! I don't want to dance 'cheek to cheek' with Luke Newton!"

Incredulous, Lindsey protested, "I just don't believe this! I've never known you to be so stubborn. Even if you don't think you'll like Luke, you could stay at the hotel and accept the prizes. And you might find out that you do like him after you meet him. Believe me, I've never met a woman who didn't."

"I'm sure," Eugenia muttered. "I've heard him telling all his women goodbye at the end of the show each day. Heaven only knows how many there are."

Lindsey laughed. "You sound jealous, Genia."

"Don't be ridiculous," Eugenia insisted. "I don't even know the man."

"So get to know him," her sister said, exasperated. "But call! Time's running out."

"No," Eugenia repeated. "And that's final!"

## Chapter Two

Luke Newton leaned back in his chair as a past hit ballad was played. He found himself wondering what this Eugenia Latrop was like. He'd been the host of a different oldies contest for three years now, and he'd had the good fortune to have each of the winners be charming companions, regardless of age or looks. He chuckled softly.

They were charming because they were fans and eager to share the spotlight with him; he had found enjoyment in that fact. They were very appreciative, and he liked that in a woman. A frown creased his brow. Ever since he and Joyce divorced three years ago, he'd been grateful for an appreciative woman.

His smile returning, he wondered what his vast, female audience would say if they knew that the role this dashing man-about-town savored the most was that of daddy. He wondered who would believe him, if he told them his favorite outing was taking Jeanie and Betsy, his six- and five-year-old daughters, to the amusement park. Dressed in old jeans and a baggy shirt, he loved putting on a hat and sunglasses and getting away from Luke Newton, disc jockey, for the entire day.

The phone rang and he was catapulted out of his thoughts. "Hello, Eugenia," he said, making his voice sound rich and warm.

On the other end of the line, Lindsey's fingers trembled visibly. "Hello, Luke," she said.

He smiled. "I knew that would be you, Eugenia. I knew you wanted to be my hostess and special guest, or you wouldn't have entered the contest, right?"

"Right," Lindsey said.

"Okay, Eugenia, what's your address?"

Lindsey gave him the address of her beach house.

"And what's your age?"

"Twenty-five."

"Birth date?"

"June 24."

"Okay, Eugenia. That checks out. You're all set as the winner. We're going to go on the air now. You *can* be properly grateful for our audience, can't you, Eugenia?" he coaxed, his voice low and encouraging. "A lot of ladies wanted to win all those fabulous gifts, so let's show our favorite radio station how pleased we are that *you* won. Okay?"

"Okay." Lindsey breathed nervously into the phone.

"Ready?"

"Yes, I think so."

"All right!" Luke said, his voice booming over the airwaves once again. "We've got a happy lady on the phone! Eugenia Latrop, tell the people how happy you are!"

"I'm—I'm thrilled!" Lindsey said obligingly, her voice rising. "I can't believe it! I'm so happy I won. I just can't wait for the Fabulous Fifties Fun Frolic. I'm just so excited. Oh, thank you, Luke!"

Eugenia rolled her eyes. Lindsey was asking for trouble with that man. Eugenia had thought her sister wasn't going to call, but two minutes before time ran out, she gave up and dialed the number.

"All right, Eugenia! You're welcome," Luke said, his voice a seductive drawl. "You stay there on the line for a minute and I'll be right back to you. Okay?"

"Okay, Luke," Lindsey said, smiling at her sister.

Eugenia had heard every word on the radio. Now Luke played a fast-paced song and returned to Lindsey. Eugenia watched as her younger sister smiled happily and chatted with the disc jockey, but she could only hear Lindsey's end of the conversation. She didn't want to admit, even to herself, that she was dying of curiosity.

When Lindsey hung up right before the record ended, Eugenia shook her head. "I can't believe you're really going to do this," she said.

Lindsey sighed dramatically. "Me, either. Oh, won't it be wonderful, Genia? All that attention, all those prizes, and me with Luke for three days! Of course the public is invited to all the events for a fee. You'll have to come and see what you're missing out on. It's all going to be fifties style—the decor, clothes, music—everything! It sounds like a real grand party!"

"The public is invited?" Eugenia repeated.

"Yes, of course. You said yourself that it's a radio-hotel promotion. There will be prizes for dance contest winners, and that kind of thing. Of course, I'll be the belle of the ball. I'll be the one doing everything with

Luke Newton, and the rest of his adoring fans can eat their hearts out. I can't wait!''

"What will Brad think?" Eugenia asked. Although she hadn't yet met the man, Lindsey had told her he was handsome and possessive.

"I hope it makes him so jealous that he proposes!" Lindsey cried. "I hope he tells me he doesn't want me to do it."

"You do?" Eugenia asked, puzzled. "I thought you wanted to be mistress of ceremonies."

"I do!" Lindsey insisted. "I have every intention of making the most of this contest, believe me, but I still hope Brad gets jealous. If he turns up, I'm going to hang all over Luke. And that's a promise."

"I really don't think *that*'s a good idea," Eugenia said.

Lindsey sighed again, this time less dramatically. "I've got to do something! How does a girl get a man to propose, Genia? I'm tired of waiting for him to ask me to marry him, and I've tried everything, short of proposing to him."

Eugenia exhaled a weary breath. "I told you, Lin, I think every man likes the chase. We may be ladies of the eighties, but I'm afraid men still do the proposing, and less frequently than ever. Why don't you back off a little and give him some time?"

"Time for what? To get away?" Lindsey asked. "Nope!" She laughed. "I wanted a summer wedding. Summer is fading fast."

"Well, at least I can understand a little better why you wanted to win the contest," Eugenia said. "You hope it might serve a purpose for you."

Lindsey frowned as she roused herself from thought. "What? What do you mean?"

"I mean it might make Brad jealous, all right. I'm relieved. I thought you honestly relished the thought of a weekend with Luke Newton."

"Oh," Lindsey said, the frown fainter now. "Yes, I'm hoping it'll serve my purpose." Her brown eyes met her sister's. "Eugenia, don't you think you have an unreasonable dislike of Luke? You've never met the man. I don't recall you being so judgmental before."

"He's just the kind of man that sets me off," Eugenia said.

Lindsey laughed. "He sets a lot of women off, big sister."

"I didn't mean like *that*," Eugenia added hastily. "I mean I don't like his kind of insufferable arrogance. It really irritates me that he acts as if every woman in the world is tuned into that station just to hear him."

Lindsey laughed again. "Eugenia, every woman in the world who's listening *is* tuned in just to hear him."

"So what's the big attraction?" Eugenia asked. "Most of the women are responding to a sexy voice. What's the man look like who goes with it?"

Lindsey kissed her fingertips in an exaggerated Italian gesture. "Fine, very fine. You don't know what you're missing out on, but it won't do me any good to tell you, since you're so adamant about not being his hostess and guest of honor."

"You're right about that," Eugenia agreed.

Shaking her head, Lindsey murmured, "It's really too bad. Still, one sister's castoff is another's treasure. You can bet I'm not foolish enough to throw away such a prize."

She took another sip of her coffee, ate a little more of her doughnut, then stood up. "I must get to work. How I envy you having the entire summer off."

"One of the perks of the educational system in this country," Eugenia said with a smile.

"Speaking of perks," Lindsey said, after taking a final sip of her coffee, "don't make any plans for tomorrow night. You and I are going out to dinner, and we're going to do it right—clothing, makeup and the whole bit. Really do the town. Okay?"

"Yes, that sounds like fun," Eugenia agreed, refusing to say "okay." She'd heard Luke Newton say it enough to last her a lifetime. "Where are we going?"

"It's a surprise," Lindsey replied. "But I guarantee you an interesting time."

"Is Brad taking us?"

"Brad?" Lindsey repeated. "Oh, no, he's not going." She picked up her purse from the living room. "See you this evening," she said, turning away. Then she glanced back over her shoulder. "Have a good day, Sis. Get out on the beach and get some sun—meet some people."

Eugenia smiled. "Yes ma'am, little sister. I'll mix and mingle as you wish."

Lindsey grinned. "I really hope so, Eugenia. And please remember that you did say you would."

Eugenia stared after her sister as the other woman closed the door behind her. Lindsey had sounded awfully serious with that last statement. Eugenia sighed. She didn't know why Lindsey was pushing her so hard to get involved with someone else. She didn't think she was ready. Not yet.


The next evening, when Lindsey and Eugenia had gotten dressed for dinner, Lindsey shook her head. "You'll never do," she declared despairingly.

"What do you mean?" Eugenia asked, trying not to feel insulted. "What's wrong with what I'm wearing? It's not exactly a burlap bag, is it?"

Lindsey chuckled. "No, and it's not exactly the hottest design of the season, either. Just wait a minute. We'll fix you right up."

To Eugenia's chagrin, her sister went to her closet and pulled out black boots, a black leather miniskirt, matching sleeveless vest and a white silk blouse.

"*This* is just the thing," Lindsey insisted. "Fortunately, we wear the same shoe size."

Laughing, Eugenia said, "You're joking, of course."

Lindsey shook her head. "I've never been more serious."

"Lin, I'm telling you right now that I'm not putting on that outfit, so don't insist," Eugenia said firmly.

"Please do it just this one time, just for me," Lin coaxed. "I promise that if you don't feel and look better than your old self, I won't ask again after tonight. Come on, Eugenia. We look like such extremes with you in that blue dress and me in a mini. Please."

Eugenia wanted to remain adamant, but relented. "Oh, why not?" she muttered to herself, even though she was perfectly satisfied with the dress she had on. But it seemed important to Lindsey, and she guessed she could try it one time, even if she felt like an utter fool at the very thought. At least she wouldn't see anyone she knew.

When she had changed, she stood staring at her image in dismay. "Lin, I really don't think so," she moaned. "Look at me!"

"I am! I am!" Lindsey said excitedly. "I never knew you had such great legs, Genia. The men'll love 'em. You know how crazy some men are about long legs."

"Oh, really, Lindsey, I feel like a—a—Well, I don't even want to say what I feel like." She looked at her shorter sister. "Your skirt is two inches longer than mine. I can't wear this."

Lindsey stepped up behind her. "Look, Genia! Look how smart and sophisticated the black looks against your fair skin. And that blouse was made for you!"

Eugenia adjusted her glasses, trying to see what her sister saw. Her face was red. She had never been one to like drawing attention to herself. That was Lindsey, not herself, but as she stared at her image, she had to admit that she'd never looked so—so sexy.

"Don't you think this is just a bit much?" she asked, feeling silly trying to believe she was attractive in the outfit, yet instinctively knowing it gave her a certain cosmopolitan look she'd never had before. "It doesn't seem quite right."

"Nonsense. I'll tell you what's wrong," Lindsey insisted. "That hair. Some people could probably get away with a chignon and a miniskirt, but not you. Let me braid it. It'll only take a minute."

Eugenia's automatic response was to resist, but she'd gone this far, so she acquiesced, even though she felt even more foolish. A French braid, for heaven's sake! She didn't care how popular they were. She felt like someone else with all these clothing and hair changes.

When they were ready, Lindsey drove down to a dining spot on Restaurant Row. Eugenia was impressed by the building, and eagerly anticipated the evening in such a posh place. After they had entered, she stood listening to the music from the nearby piano bar while Lindsey told the host at the front desk that they had reservations for dinner.

"Take your glasses off," Lindsey suddenly hissed as they started to follow the maître d'.

"Are you crazy?" Eugenia whispered back. "I can't see much of anything without them."

"Please, just for a few minutes," Lindsey said urgently.

Shaking her head in disbelief, Eugenia complied. Boy, would she be glad when this night was over! She'd think twice about going *anywhere* with Lindsey again, and that was a promise!

The maître d' led them toward a cozy, corner table where a sandy-haired man of medium height and build was sitting. Even without her glasses, Eugenia could see him in detail at this distance. He was dressed in a pale blue suit with a blue- and white-striped tie. She found herself thinking that he looked rather debonair and attractive.

As they drew nearer, she realized even with her fuzzy vision that he was smiling at her. His gaze roved over first herself, then Lindsey, but not in an insulting way.

Eugenia nervously decided that his appraisal was more from curiosity than anything else, but then what else could she expect in this getup? She blushed from the top of her head to the tips of her toes. She wasn't used to getting much male attention. It *had* to be this darned outfit! She was suddenly uneasy at his casual assessment of her. He stared at them almost as though he was expecting to meet them, Eugenia realized. His smile broadened in appreciation as he let his gaze drift over her clothing and back up to her face a second time.

Quickly looking at Lindsey, Eugenia was tempted to suggest that they ask the maître d' to seat them elsewhere. She was going to be uncomfortable if this flirty man stared at them all evening. She was acutely aware of him sitting there all alone.

With a shock, she realized that they were being led right to his table. She glanced at the maître d', wondering if he realized his mistake, but when he announced, "Your table, ladies," Eugenia somehow knew that this was no mistake. This was something Lindsey had arranged. She sensed it.

Unexpectedly, another man appeared out of nowhere, strolling toward the table. He was about five feet seven inches tall, had red hair and weighed a little more than he should have. Eugenia glanced from one man to the other and her imagination ran wild. The shorter, chubby man just had to be Luke Newton, and the other one was no doubt Lindsey's handsome Brad! Darn her sister! She had tricked her!

She sucked in her breath when the lean man stood up and extended his hand. "Ladies," he said in a deep, sexy, familiar voice, "this is a surprise—a welcome one. Which one of you is Eugenia?"

Eugenia turned startled eyes to Lindsey, but Lindsey was already introducing her. "Eugenia Latrop, this is Luke Newton. And I'm her sister, Lindsey," she said, smiling warmly at him.

Luke took Eugenia's hand in his, and she inanely told herself that *he* was the disc jockey, not the chubby man. Her mind was swirling in confusion. Although he wasn't a very big man himself—about five feet ten with a wiry, lean frame—he definitely was handsome. Eugenia suspected that he was either an athlete or runner.

"How do you do?" he murmured politely, in a voice that sent chills over her skin. Oddly, the deep, husky voice fitted him.

"Fine," she said. It was an outright fib. She wasn't fine at all. She was confused and angry. If Lindsey had made arrangements to meet Luke Newton here, she could at least have said so. Eugenia wouldn't have come. Now Luke knew that she was the one who had won the trip.

Luke turned to Lindsey. "And how are you?"

She laughed. "I'm great. Just great. It's so exciting to meet you. I've listened to you the entire three years I've lived here."

Luke turned to the other man. "Well, maybe you've heard this man, too. This is Jordan Weaver, another disc jockey from the station."

He gazed at Jordan, mischief dancing in his eyes. "I suppose you're going to insist that I ask you to join us, since there are two beautiful ladies this evening." His tone was dry, but there was laughter in his voice.

Jordan shook his head in an exaggerated manner. "I wouldn't *dream* of intruding," he said. "I just wanted to take a little peek. Damn you, Luke, you lucky dog! When is the contest winner ever going to be a lady in her nineties with blue hair?"

Both men laughed. Unexpectedly, Jordan took Eugenia's hand, kissed it, then Lindsey's, and walked away, shaking his head as if in dismay.

"*That* was Jordan Weaver?" Lindsey asked, obviously disappointed.

"The man in the flesh," Luke said. "Apparently you've listened to him. He's a super guy and a real funny man on the air, isn't he?"

Lindsey smiled noncommittally, but it was all too apparent she wasn't impressed. Eugenia couldn't help but think that if Jordan had been as handsome as Luke, Lindsey would have liked him just fine. Well, *she*'d liked him, she thought defensively. He probably wasn't arrogant on the air like Luke Newton.

"I'll have to listen to him," Eugenia said. "He seems like a very nice man."

Luke studied her for a moment and nodded.

"We're from Lynchburg, Virginia originally," Lindsey said, drawing Luke's attention to herself. "Actually, Eugenia still lives there, so isn't it amazing that she won the contest? She's just visiting," she said with a laugh.

Eugenia realized that Lindsey was both nervous and flustered, but then, so was she! This was all wrong. How was Lindsey going to pretend she was the winner, now that she'd given their real names?

"Eugenia's only here for a few weeks," Lindsey continued, chattering brightly, "so isn't it incredible that you drew her name?"

Luke looked at Eugenia again. "Yes, incredible," he said. "I'm delighted to have such good luck." His hazel eyes roved over her face. "You're very pretty."

Frankly, she wasn't his type, he thought to himself. She was too trendy in that black leather, even if he did have to admit that she had gorgeous, long legs, but she would work just fine as hostess and guest of honor for the Fifties Frolic. The last thing he needed was a shy, retiring little flower to fade into the woodwork every time he needed some help introducing a dance, rock group or contest winner.

Eugenia didn't feel pretty, and she didn't like this smoothie telling her she was. She was sure the casual compliment meant nothing to him. It was part and parcel of his packaging, she told herself, as was his suave appearance. He was a product put together to win fans for the radio station.

But then she was packaged for the evening, too, by Lindsey. She silently swore to herself that her sister would never hear the end of this, if they lived to be those old ladies in their nineties with blue hair that Jordan had mentioned.

"Thank you for the compliment," she said stiffly. Her tone was not lost on Luke.

He raised his brows slightly as he met her eyes. Then he pulled out a chair for her. "Please sit down. Ladies, I'm delighted to have this chance to get to know you— both of you—before the weekend of the frolic. It loosens the inhibitions a bit and makes both of us more relaxed."

He glanced at Eugenia, who looked as if she'd never relaxed in her life. There'd been a definite change since they'd arrived at his table, and he had a feeling that it was going to work to his disadvantage. "Usually," he added.

He wondered what was going on here. His sixth sense told him that something was amiss. This wasn't the first time someone else had come with the winner to break the ice, but this pretty blonde didn't exactly seem elated about being here. In fact, she didn't seem pleased at all.

Well, he told himself, this would be a first if she'd changed her mind. He had anticipated it at some point with one of these contests. Most women who entered never actually imagined that they had a real chance of winning.

He felt a slight surge of disappointment wash through him, and he wasn't even sure why. As he'd noted, Eugenia wasn't his type, even though she really was quite pretty. Maybe it was plain old male ego; he didn't know. He did know that he didn't like the cold shoulder he was getting from her.

"If you'll just excuse me a moment," Lindsey said, as Luke pulled out her chair. "I need to run to the ladies' room. Nerves," she added hastily.

Luke smiled and told himself that perhaps it was a shame this sister hadn't won. She was quite pretty herself in that dark, dramatic way of hers. In fact, he realized that she reminded him of his ex-wife, Joyce. That in itself ought to be reason enough to shy away from Lindsey.

He looked at Eugenia. There was something about her reserved, haughty look, despite the modern clothes, that made him want to break down her barriers. He'd like to see her smile, hear her laugh.

He watched her eyes widen in alarm as her sister hurried away from the table. Seating himself beside her, he murmured, "Well, here we are. Are you excited about winning the contest?"

She turned her big, blue eyes in his direction. "No, I'm not," she said bluntly. "And I'm not going to be your cohost."

"You're not going to be my cohost at the Fifties Frolic?" Luke repeated, as if unable to comprehend what Eugenia had said. He realized how disappointed he was, when she verbalized his suspicions.

"Yes, that's what I said," Eugenia answered coolly. How dare Lindsey do this to her! She looked in the direction where her sister had disappeared. She didn't find this amusing at all.

"Why not?" Luke asked. He shrugged, trying to act nonchalant. "It's going to be fun, and has lots of benefits."

"Listen, Mr. Newton," Eugenia said, "I never entered that contest. Lindsey did. She submitted both our names. *She*'s the one who wants to do it, and I think she's the one who should."

Luke looked down at his glass of water, hesitated a moment, then took a swallow. His throat was unusually dry. His chest felt tight. He wanted to tell this woman that she had no right to reject him like this; yes, reject, he repeated to himself. He was taking this much too personally.

"You won the contest," he said casually as he set down the glass.

"Mr. Newton—"

"Please," he interrupted. "Let's not be so formal. It's Luke. Lucas, actually," he added with a grin, "but everyone calls me Luke."

Eugenia could feel her temper rise. She glanced toward the ladies' room again. What was keeping Lindsey?

Luke reached out and touched her hand. "Eugenia."

Her eyes met his as he drawled out the syllables in her name in that sexy way.

"You don't mind if I call you Eugenia, do you?" he asked, holding her gaze, now that he had her attention. "It's a lovely name. It sounds rather old-fashioned to me."

It is, Eugenia thought to herself. Like me. She didn't feel comfortable in this situation at all. She drew in a steadying breath.

"I don't really think you'll be using my name," she said. "This is all a mistake. Now, when Lindsey returns, the two of you can get to know each other and I'll just run along."

Luke reached out for her hand again; this time he captured it in his. "What's your hurry, Eugenia?" he murmured. "I'd really like to get to know you."

She reached up to adjust her glasses in a betrayingly nervous gesture, then realized that she wasn't even wearing them. She had dropped them into her purse, but at the moment she didn't want to see any more than she had to. Her blurry vision was a godsend in this awful time of embarrassment.

"Listen, Luke—" She tested the name on her tongue and found that she liked it. It suited this man in some indefinable way; she wasn't sure why. It, too, was an old-fashioned name, but he was hardly an old-fashioned man—not with his scores of female fans.

She tried again. "Listen, Luke, I'm sure this has never happened before, but no one need know. Lindsey and I had agreed to say she was Eugenia Lindsey Latrop and let her accept as contest winner."

He squeezed her fingers. "You were going to lie to me, Eugenia?"

"Not exactly lie," she muttered, feeling herself sinking deeper and deeper. Why did he make it sound like such a sin? She wanted to wrench her hand free of his, yet couldn't seem to find the strength.

"Then what exactly?" he murmured.

The wine steward stepped up to the table. "Will you be having wine with dinner, sir?"

"Eugenia?"

She looked away again, wondering what on earth was keeping Lindsey. "Fine," she said in a tight voice. "Whatever you want."

"Oh?" Blurred though her vision was, she thought she saw Luke Newton's hazel eyes sparkle.

"Whatever?" he repeated.

"Whatever wine," she added wryly, pulling her hand from his. He really was the most impossible man!

He grinned at her, then ordered wine. As soon as the wine steward left, a waiter walked over to the table. Luke glanced at Eugenia, then back at the waiter.

"I don't think we're ready to order yet," he said. "Please come back in a few minutes."

Eugenia seized the moment to stand up. "I'll go look for Lindsey," she said. She rushed away before Luke could comment. She would go see about Lindsey, all right, then she'd leave. She didn't want any part of this occasion!

# Chapter Three

Eugenia had to ask a waiter where the rest room was, and when he pointed down a long hall, she was grateful that Luke couldn't see her. She rummaged in her purse for her glasses, but in her agitation couldn't seem to find them. Squinting, she stared at the pair of pale blue doors. Both had figures on them.

Suddenly, firm male fingers clasped her arm. "You wanted the ladies' room, I believe," Luke Newton's deep voice murmured.

Eugenia nodded. He turned her around and opened a door for her. God help me! she thought. She'd almost gone into the men's room, and probably wouldn't even have known the difference!

The moment she entered the rest room, an attendant asked, "Are you Miss Latrop?"

Eugenia muttered a yes, instinctively knowing that she was about to hear of more trouble.

"A young lady left this note for you." She handed Eugenia a white square that looked like a cocktail napkin.

"Darn!" Eugenia mumbled as she rummaged in her purse again, hopelessly searching for her glasses. Her face burning with shame, she peered at the note, but it was just a bunch of fuzzy words. Lindsey's flamboyant handwriting was difficult enough to read anytime, but all crammed and cramped together on the little square of paper, it was impossible for Eugenia.

"I'm sorry," she said to the attendant, "but do you see my glasses anywhere in my purse?" She held the big bag open.

"No, I don't," the woman said after dutifully searching through the contents.

Eugenia exhaled. "Would you mind terribly reading the note for me?" she asked, thinking that she'd love to sink through the floor forever. She knew already that she wasn't going to like the message.

The attendant unfolded the square napkin. "Dear Eugenia," she read obediently in a singsong voice, then stopped. "Actually, I already peeked. Did you really win that radio contest?" she asked excitedly. "With Luke Newton? Everybody I know entered it, and I never expected to meet the winner. Is it really you? You're a celebrity!"

Eugenia muttered something totally inaudible, retrieved the piece of paper and rushed back out of the bathroom.

"Damn!" she cursed beneath her breath, clutching the square, trying frantically to see exactly what it said. Suddenly she crashed into Luke, who had been waiting for her.

"I'm sorry," she cried, looking up at him with startled, blue eyes.

"I didn't mind," he drawled, holding her shoulders a moment too long. He took her arm. "You're upset," he murmured, his deep voice full of concern. "Is something wrong? Has something happened to your sister?"

Drawing in a steadying breath, Eugenia tried to control her anger. "No, I think not," she said. "There was this note for me."

"Oh? What does it say?" he asked, puzzled.

Her face flaming, Eugenia held it up again and looked at it, knowing she couldn't read it and not knowing what to tell him. To her chagrin, Luke slipped it from her shaking fingers and began to read aloud.

"Dear Eugenia,
See, I told you Luke Newton wasn't so bad. I know you'll get along fine with him, so I left. Now don't be angry with me over this. Please don't say no. I'll be there at the Fabulous Fifties Fun Frolic with you, so please accept the prize and be hostess. I just know it'll be wonderful! I swear I would have let fate take its course if *I* had won, but since I didn't, please accept."

Feeling like a total idiot, Eugenia stiffened as she listened to Luke.

"Eugenia, is this note right?" Luke drawled. "Do you think I'm *bad*? And just what does that mean? Aren't you judging a man who you don't know rather harshly? Bad?"

"I—I—oh, damn," Eugenia muttered. She forced herself to smile. After all, Luke Newton wasn't responsible for this mess just because he'd selected her name for the contest. Lindsey should never have entered for her.

She looked at his face, and even with hazy vision, she couldn't help noticing again how appealing he was. Long, thick, brown lashes shielded his eyes. His nose was straight, and his mouth was full and well shaped. He had a male model's sculpted jawline and a well-defined body. Eugenia guessed that he was about thirty-four, but couldn't really tell.

"I didn't say—or mean—bad like *bad*," she said, literally at a loss for words. All she wanted to do was leave, as Lindsey had done. She'd been mortified enough in one night to last a lifetime. She despised being manipulated, even if it was done with love and good intentions.

"How did you say—or mean—*bad*?" he asked, and she could hear the laughter in his voice. "Like bad, as in real cool, or bad as in not good?"

Before she could start stammering again, he took her arm. "Let's go back to the table and get this straightened out," he said.

"I don't think that's necessary," she said, trying not to make things even worse. She was sure he had more than his share of female attention; she didn't want to be part of the crowd. "As I said, this has all been a mistake. Lindsey entered me in the contest and she's trying to persuade me to go. She really wants me to."

"I want you to go, too," Luke said, and Eugenia was surprised by the soft tone of his voice. "Why won't you? I promise I'm not bad-bad, you know."

Eugenia found herself looking away. Lindsey's comment that Luke really wasn't so bad seemed true at that moment. It was hard for Eugenia to remember how she'd disliked this man on the radio. In fact, she felt like laughing at the way he kept trying to explain that he wasn't bad.

He took her hand again and led her back to the table. "Sit down, Eugenia. Let's talk about it," he coaxed. "The least we can do is have dinner." He indicated her glass. "Your wine has already been poured."

Every instinct told Eugenia to leave right now, but her feet seemed firmly planted where they were. When Luke came over to pull out her chair, she sat down.

When the waiter came back to the table, Luke murmured, "I know you haven't had a chance to look at the menu, Eugenia. May I order for you? They have wonderful seafood here. You do like seafood, don't you?" he asked, as if it had just occurred to him that she might not.

She nodded. "Yes."

"Then shall I order?"

She nodded again, feeling out of control. Maybe he was trying to be nice, she told herself, but she felt as if she were being manipulated again. She was here with a man she didn't want to be with, and now she was going to eat a meal he'd ordered. Maybe, she thought with alarm, he realized that she was nearly blind as a bat, and he felt sorry for her. That made her feel even worse.

When Luke had placed the order, he smiled at her. "I don't understand," he said simply. "What's the problem here? Why does Lindsey have to persuade you to come to the frolic with me?"

Eugenia met his steady gaze and was tempted to simply blurt out the truth to him. She'd already told him she didn't want to go, but could she tell him that she didn't like him? And was that even the truth, now that she'd met him? This man didn't seem as obnoxious as the one on the radio. It was as though he had a split personality.

Before she could think of a reply, he continued speaking. "You're shy, aren't you?"

"No!" she retorted, but of course, he'd hit the truth. Despite her teaching career and spending lots of time with the students' parents, she really was somewhat introverted and felt more comfortable with the children and the elderly people at the nursing home.

Lindsey had been the star in their cosmos, right from the day she was born, but Eugenia had never resented her younger sister. In fact, she loved Lin so much that that was the reason she'd decided she wanted four children of her own, and why she wanted to teach. Still, her shyness wasn't the primary reason why she didn't want to go with Luke Newton.

"Listen," he said, leaning closer to her. She could feel his warm breath on her face. "I don't bite. I take part in this contest every year with ladies of all ages, from all walks of life, and no one has ever said she didn't have a good time. You won't say it either, I promise."

There it was, Eugenia told herself; there was the arrogant side of him she'd heard on the radio. "I don't want to burst your bubble, Luke," she said dryly, "but I simply don't want to do this with you."

Luke seemed taken aback for a moment. Surely he'd figured out what the problem was, he thought. However, Eugenia was so adamant that maybe he was wrong. Oh, not that he didn't think she wasn't shy, but she sounded very much like a lady who really didn't want to be with *him*.

He tried to smile, but he hadn't felt so rejected since Joyce had walked out. He was really bothered by the fact that this pretty blonde didn't want to take part in such a wonderful contest.

"Why not?" he asked gently. "You don't even know me. Why are you so set against accepting?"

Eugenia chewed on her lower lip, then realized what she was doing and freed it. That was a habit of Lindsey's that she particularly disliked. She was still debating what she could tell Luke when their salads arrived. She started eating hers to keep herself occupied.

Across the table from her, Luke murmured, "Are you afraid to go through with it, Eugenia? Is it stage fright? Fear of the limelight?"

Her gaze darted up to his. "Really, Mr. Newton, you underestimate me," she said in an icy tone. "I'm not some cowering little schoolmarm. I'm simply not interested in being your cohost for some crazy early rock 'n' roll weekend, no matter what the so-called perks of such an event. I don't care that it's loaded with extras, you're the escort, et cetera."

Luke leaned back in his chair. He sensed that there was more to this than met the eye. Or was he only hoping to salvage his own pride? This woman was speaking like one who'd had a bad experience and never intended to repeat it. Or was he reading something into nothing, because he wanted to find the key to Eugenia, so he could convince her to be his hostess?

What made her so defensive? So adamant about not participating, regardless of all his coaxing? Was it really him? His own self-esteem couldn't accept that. He didn't want to believe it! Was it something as simple as a bad public experience that had embarrassed her? Or was it maybe a man in her past?

His own divorce had changed his life; he'd been devastated when Joyce told him she didn't like being married to a stuffy, college communications instructor, living her life with boring academic people.

Funny. She hadn't minded his career and his academic friends at all when she'd been a student in his class, trying to get his exclusive attention. But then, everything had changed after the birth of their daughters, Jeanie and Betsy. Luke was well aware that he had changed. He savored his role of family man. He'd thought Joyce enjoyed being a housewife. She had dropped out of school when the two of them married.

He took a sip of his wine. That was all water under the bridge. He was a far cry from that college teacher now. And a different woman had entered his life. Another one who didn't want to be in it, he thought wryly.

It suddenly occurred to him that maybe it was something as simple as Eugenia being married to a husband who didn't like the idea. If that was the case, why didn't she simply say so?

"Are you married?" he asked.

"No," she said too quickly.

"Engaged?"

"No, if it's any of your business."

"Man in your life right now?"

"Really!" Eugenia cried. "I think you already know I'm single. That's part of the contest rules, isn't it?"

"No," he said, "it isn't. Anyway, being single doesn't mean you don't have a man in your life."

He realized in that moment that he didn't want her to be involved with someone, and that his reaction was absurd. He didn't even know the woman, and she didn't want to know him!

His gaze met Eugenia's. As he watched her, he decided to take a different tack. He had to conclude that she didn't like him, despite not even knowing him. He wanted to change that. He didn't know if it was the challenge or ego, but he was as determined to find a way to persuade this woman to take part in the party as she was not to participate.

"What do you do for a living?" he asked.

When Eugenia met his eyes again, she saw that he was smiling at her.

"I teach grade school."

He grinned. A teacher! "So you *are* a schoolmarm."

Well, she'd backed herself right into that corner. What could she say?

"Yes."

"Do you like your job?"

For the first time, Luke saw those pretty, blue eyes of hers glow. "Yes, I love it."

He nodded. "I love mine, too."

"I can tell when I hear you on the radio," she said a little pointedly.

"Meaning?" he asked.

Eugenia shrugged. "Meaning that you seem to really love your work and your audience—especially the ladies."

He heard the censure in her voice, but wasn't about to admit it. He was well aware of his reputation as a ladies' man; it was part of a carefully cultivated image that allowed him to be a different person when he was on the radio. In real life, he was a one-woman man. At least he would be if he could find that special woman.

"Then you'll understand why I don't want to let my audience—or the station—down," he said in a soft, seductive voice. "I do have a certain reputation to keep up, Eugenia."

He reached across and took her free hand before she could jerk it away. "I'd take it as a personal favor if you'd accept as contest winner. Can you imagine how humiliating it will be for me to have to announce, two days after I've picked the winner, that she can't come after all, and I have to choose someone else? I've *never* had to do that, and this isn't the only contest I conduct, you know. It's the year's biggest, but we have contests constantly.''

Eugenia exhaled tiredly as she pried her fingers from his. She should have known that he would be worried about his image. ''All you have to say is that I'm ill, or that I've had an accident,'' she told him.

He shook his head. ''I couldn't do that.''

''Why not?''

''I never lie,'' he said.

''Oh, for heaven's sake!'' she cried. ''Make an exception this time—for your reputation.''

The waiter stepped up to the table with her food, and she started at his sudden appearance. ''Your meal, madam,'' he said solicitously. She was aware that Luke was watching her, and she defiantly met his eyes.

''You're very nervous, aren't you?'' he murmured, uncaring that the waiter overheard the conversation. ''I really think you need to take the role of cohost of the frolic. It'll bring you out of yourself, I guarantee. It'll be a good experience for you. I really do believe you're shy, Eugenia, despite that foxy outfit.''

Her face hot with embarrassment, Eugenia glanced at the waiter, who seemed oblivious to what was being said. He served Luke, then vanished as quietly as he'd arrived. Damn Lin and this outfit! she told herself before directing her anger at Luke.

''What is it about the word *no* that you can't comprehend?'' she asked irritably. ''Do you need a cue card? I'm *not* taking part in that frolic!''

Luke was fast losing his patience. He wanted to speak as sharply to her as she had to him, but sensed that would never work. The problem was, he was at a loss to decide how best to handle this situation.

"The station accepted your entry in good faith, Eugenia," he said calmly. "And you did call and accept. We had no way of knowing the fraud involved."

"Fraud?" she repeated, blue eyes wide.

"Wasn't that what it was?" he asked solemnly, gazing intently at her.

Eugenia attempted to adjust her missing glasses again, and when she realized they weren't there, she tapped her nose nervously. "Oh, how did I ever get in this mess?" she asked aloud.

"Your sister entered you in a contest," Luke said, his tone slightly mocking. He surmised that Lindsey was the one who had called and accepted, too. He suspected Eugenia wouldn't have mustered any enthusiasm for the radio audience, even if her life had depended upon it. Or his.

When she met his eyes, he said persuasively, "I'll owe you one if you'll just agree to go with me. Please say yes. It's only one weekend out of your life, and you can't imagine the humiliation it would save me. I promise you that I'll see to it that you aren't uncomfortable, that you have a good time. I'll even include your sister in whatever I can, if that'll make you more comfortable. I've never agreed to such a thing before," he said emphatically.

That sexy, seductive voice washed over her, temporarily mesmerizing Eugenia. She didn't want to give in and go, but Luke was succeeding in making her feel guilty. The word humiliation hit a nerve.

And she knew, too, that anything Lindsey could be included in would thrill her, although at the moment she didn't know why she cared in the least what would make her sister happy!

Against her better judgment, she heard herself say in an exasperated tone, "Oh, all right. I'll do it, but I'm not happy about it. You won't be, either," she added abruptly. "Really, I'm not what I seem tonight. You'd be much better off with Lindsey."

Luke leaned back in his chair and smiled. "I'm happy," he said a trifle smugly. And he meant to see that she was able to say the same thing when the Fifties Fun Frolic was over.

"Well, that makes one of us, anyway," she said, aware that she wasn't being at all gracious about this. She felt as though she'd been coerced by both him and Lindsey. She vowed that she would take Lindsey to task when she got back home!

"Mmm," Luke said, biting into a succulent shrimp, "—delicious. Which reminds me, I'm sure you'll love the food at the Fifties Frolic. It's only one of the fantastic things about the weekend."

"So tell me the others," Eugenia said with a resigned sigh.

Luke enthusiastically launched into the things they would do at the resort hotel. "Each night will have a different theme. For example, the first night is a fifties beach party, right on the beach with a wiener roast. We're actually hiring two original fifties beach bands to provide the music."

He saw Eugenia's eyes sparkle with interest and rushed on. "The second night will be kind of a teenybopper thing, with all the guests wearing fifties teen clothes. The food will be hamburgers, fries, et cetera, but the third night will be the grand finale. The last night is going to be fifties formal, with a well-known band and a sit-down dinner.''

Eugenia felt a small thrill of excitement. The party really *did* sound like fun. Under other circumstances—

She brushed the thought aside and took a sip of wine. There were no other circumstances. She was going to guest-host a nostalgia party with disc jockey Luke Newton. She was waiting in line for his attention after heaven only knew how many other women!

''Eugenia.''

She looked up quickly when he drawled her name in that sexy husky way. Eugenia felt the shivers race over her skin, and hated her reaction to his seductive tone. He had an amazing voice, and he used it to his best advantage.

''Yes?'' she asked brusquely, pursing her lips in annoyance, more at herself than Luke.

He grinned at her, knowing she was determined to keep her distance, even though she'd agreed to go through with the weekend.

''Does the frolic sound okay to you?''

She nodded. ''It sounds okay—all right,'' she corrected herself, already having decided never to use the word okay again.

Luke searched her face for some emotion betraying more than that the plans for the party sounded all right. A lot of time and expense had gone into it; everyone else thought it was going to be the big shindig of the season.

If he'd read Eugenia correctly, she'd been excited when he talked about the party and all the events planned for each night. It really was a great undertaking, and it had done a lot for the station and the hotel. That, and the fact that he was known as such a ladies' man.

He really did love the ladies, he told himself, watching Eugenia Latrop. Usually they loved him. This would be a different experience. He would have to work harder to win this woman's approval. But he fully intended to do it. No matter how long it took.

"Aren't you going to try your shrimp?" he asked, his eyes all innocence as they met hers.

Eugenia obediently picked up a large shrimp and bit into it.

"Is it okay?" Luke asked.

"It's good," she answered honestly.

In fact, it was better than that, she admitted to herself. It was delicious. She didn't know why she couldn't let herself tell him that. Maybe it was because he had ordered the meal, and she didn't want to go overboard approving of his choice.

"I'm glad," he said softly.

Eugenia glanced at him again. He used that incredible voice like a musical instrument. She wondered if he knew what a gift he had. He could command attention simply by altering his tone, speaking in a lower voice or more gently. She watched him smile at her, and realized that he knew his power over women.

That only made her more determined not to succumb to his charm. And yes, she admitted, he *did* have charm. But she would leave the discovery of his attributes to his other women.

She didn't like to share. Especially when what she was sharing was a man. She'd learned that the hard way with Daniel. She didn't need to repeat the lesson.

When they had finished eating, Luke asked Eugenia, "Would you like to have a drink at the piano bar?"

Eugenia shook her head. She had no intentions of staying a moment longer with Luke tonight. "No, thanks. I'd better get home. Lindsey will wonder what's keeping me."

Luke chuckled. "I believe she knows, don't you?"

"No. She couldn't be sure I'd stay, and if I did, she knew it was only for dinner—nothing more. There'll be nothing more," Eugenia stated.

Luke smiled and stood up. "Whatever the lady says. Ready, then?"

"Yes, thank you."

When they went by the reception desk, a young man held up a pair of glasses. "Are these yours, perchance, madam? Someone found them on the floor."

Eugenia wished with all her heart that she could say no, but the truth of the matter was that she needed her glasses. They were her favorite pair and like an old friend.

"Yes," she said crisply. "Thank you."

For a moment she couldn't decide whether she should shove them into her purse or wear them, then she slipped them on. She hadn't had much luck putting them into her purse the first time, obviously, and she did need to see. Thankfully, Luke didn't say a word. Outside, he led her to a low-slung black sports car. Somehow she had expected no less of Luke Newton. The racy car fitted his image to a tee.

After he'd opened the door for her, Eugenia slid inside, acutely aware of Luke watching her. With her glasses, she could see clearly just how handsome he really was, though she hadn't had any problem realizing that, even without them.

She settled into the deep, plush seat and looked up at him. He gave her a smile before he closed the door. Eugenia stared straight ahead and promised herself that she wouldn't return his contagious smile. She was tempted to take off her glasses so she wouldn't be so aware of him, but somehow knew that wouldn't help.

He seated himself behind the wheel. "Sure you won't have a drink somewhere?" he asked.

"Positive."

She didn't look at him, not even when she heard his husky laugh. She was grateful when he turned the radio dial and classical piano music spilled into the car, filling up the emptiness.

They rode along for a few minutes, both listening to the radio. Then Luke asked, "Are you going to tell me where you live?"

Eugenia looked at him with wide eyes. "Didn't you ask Lindsey over the phone?"

Luke let his gaze linger on her face before he returned his attention to the road. So it *was* Lindsey who'd called, he told himself. Well, he'd already suspected as much. There was no point in bringing it up now.

The same was true of the glasses. He was tempted to ask her why she hadn't mentioned that they were missing. He was also tempted to tell her that he was half-blind without his contacts—but he let the temptation pass.

"I know I'm something, Eugenia, however even I can't remember an address I repeated only one time," he drawled.

She allowed herself a small laugh. "No, I suppose not," she conceded as she gave him the address.

"Ah, yes," he said. "I do remember. It's right on the beach. Lucky you."

He knew the area well. In fact, he'd once lived in the same neighborhood, although he hadn't had a place right on the beach. He'd lived a street over from Lindsey's home and up several houses.

Although it seemed like decades ago, it had been little more than three years. He'd considered himself very fortunate to get a place in that section of town. It was a premium area, quiet and established and away from the influx of tourists.

"Lucky Lindsey," Eugenia corrected him, interrupting Luke's thoughts.

"Aren't you lucky, too?" he asked, gazing at her again.

She managed a small smile. "Not too often."

She jumped when he reached over and squeezed her leg. "Well, guess what, Eugenia? I think your luck has changed."

"Oh?" she said, reaching down to brush his hand away, but to her chagrin, he moved it before she could make a point.

She found herself thinking a weekend with Luke might be more than she'd bargained for. "Why do you think my luck has changed?"

He laughed deep and low. "Because you won the contest with all those prizes *and* three days with me. How lucky can one woman get?"

"How lucky indeed," she muttered.

Just when she was trying to decide that Luke Newton wasn't so bad, he had to come up with something like that. It was going to be a long weekend, one she suspected she'd regret ever agreeing to.

When Luke parked in the driveway, Eugenia opened the door herself. "Good night," she said. "I'll see you week after next at the station."

"Eugenia," he drawled.

"What?" She was already getting out of the car.

"I'll see you before then."

"I think not," she said.

Luke sighed. She really was going to be difficult. "Whatever you say, Eugenia. Good night."

He watched as she went up the driveway. The abbreviated skirt hugged her hips, giving him a delicious view of her long legs. Her nylons looked golden under the lamp that lighted the entrance. Luke found himself thinking again how pretty Eugenia was. Just because he didn't like the blatantly sexy costume didn't mean he didn't respond to it.

"She's going to be difficult," he murmured, "but worth it. Definitely worth it."

## Chapter Four

After Eugenia vanished inside the house, Luke gunned the motor and pulled away. Eugenia peered out the blinds to make sure he'd left before going to confront Lindsey. To her irritation, she found another note from her sister. This one was on the refrigerator, and with her glasses she could read it all too clearly.

> Gone with Brad to dinner. Be back late. Hope you agreed to accept as contest winner.
>
> > Love you, Lindsey.

"Yes, I agreed, darn it!" Eugenia said aloud. "And I hope you're happy now!"

She ripped the note from the refrigerator and went down the hall to her bedroom. She couldn't think of anything she'd rather do than curl up in bed and go to sleep. The night had been a trial, to say the least.

When she'd stripped off her sister's clothes and put on a simple, brief gown, she slid under the sheet and lay on her side. After a few minutes, she switched to another position. She found that didn't help. Sleep was elusive. She strained to hear sounds of Lindsey coming home, and told herself her sister's absence was the only reason she couldn't sleep, but she knew she was lying.

The truth was that in spite of all she'd said, she was as excited about the contest as she was nervous. She was excited about the frolic, and yes, she had to admit it, no matter how it annoyed her, she was excited about Luke Newton. He hadn't been quite what she expected.

But then in some ways he had, she told herself. He was still the arrogant voice on the radio. His husky laughter echoed in her ears. She closed her eyes.

She heard it again. That amazing, sexy voice. Only this time, he was calling her name in that seductive drawl of his. She drifted off to sleep before she discovered what he wanted.

When Eugenia got up the next morning, she found Lindsey in the kitchen, happily eating her usual breakfast of coffee and sweet rolls.

"Good morning," Eugenia said, startling her sister, who had been singing along with a song on the radio again.

"Oh! Good morning," Lindsey said, her face animated. "Well, what happened? Did you agree to help Luke host the fifties party?"

Eugenia wasn't about to let Lindsey off that easily. She'd slept poorly; she couldn't seem to stop thinking about the contest—and Luke Newton. She didn't know how she'd let him persuade her to participate.

"And how was your evening, little sister, after you ran off, leaving me with that disc jockey?" Eugenia asked with an edge in her voice.

"Wasn't he delightful?" Lindsey asked.

Eugenia heard the hope in Lindsey's voice. "Delightful?" she repeated. "How about self-inflated? If he'd been an inner tube, he would have exploded! Lindsey," she murmured, "how could you do that to me? You know I don't want to host that darned party with Luke Newton!"

"You didn't refuse?" Lindsey asked anxiously. "You *didn't*, Eugenia!"

"Just what did you really expect me to do, after you left that dreadful little square of paper in the bathroom, telling me you'd gone and that I should accept?" Eugenia demanded. "Did you really think that was a decent thing to do?"

"It was the only thing I could think of to get you two alone," Lindsey said, a pout on her lips. "It wasn't such an awful idea, was it?"

"Awful?" Eugenia cried. "Awful! It was worse than that! When you *insisted* that I take off my glasses, I managed to drop them instead of put them in my purse. I couldn't even read the damn note, and the attendant in the rest room embarrassed me by having already read it and calling me a celebrity."

Lindsey laughed. "I think that's charming."

"I'm glad you do," Eugenia retorted, "because that's not even half of it! I rushed out of the bathroom, clutching the note, still not able to read it, and I crashed right into Luke!"

Lindsey giggled again. "I'm sorry I left. It sounds *very* entertaining to me."

"It was, let me assure you," Eugenia said dryly. "Luke was concerned about you, while I was wanting to break your neck! *He* took the note and read it—aloud!"

Lindsey hooted with uncontrolled laughter. "What a story. I had no idea! I love it!"

"Lin, it's not funny," Eugenia insisted.

When Lindsey saw the serious expression in her sister's eyes, she tried to stifle her laughter, but the truth of the matter was that she found it funny. She'd had no idea all that had gone on.

"I'm sorry, Genia," she apologized between giggles, "but it really does sound funny. I wish I'd heard the conversation."

"It wasn't funny," Eugenia cried. "Think about how you would have felt under the circumstances."

"Honest, I'm sorry, but it is funny," Lindsey said, starting to laugh again.

Eugenia shook her head, then she, too, succumbed to her sister's infectious laughter as Lindsey broke into a fit of giggles. Now that she was safely home and distanced from the evening, Eugenia could see the humorous side of the fiasco.

"Back to the critical question," Lindsey said, trying to stop giggling. "You did accept, didn't you?"

Seating herself across from her sister, Eugenia decided not to let the younger woman off so easily. "I should have refused, shouldn't I? I mean under the circumstances, I think it was only right that I refuse."

"Genia! You didn't!"

"Lin, you had no right to do that to me—any of it, enter me in the contest, leave me with Luke. I didn't come here for you to manipulate me into something like this. You deliberately set me up with Luke Newton. You're hoping I'll become personally interested in him."

Lindsey laughed openly. "Wherever did you get such an idea? You don't think Luke gets involved with the women who win the contests, do you? Why, that wouldn't benefit the station at all. In fact, it would probably be scandalous. The women don't have to be single to win, you know."

"I really don't know what the man does," Eugenia retorted. "But I can guess. You've heard him for three years. You must know that he sounds like a rogue."

"So?" Lindsey said. "I didn't say you *have* to become interested in him, for heaven's sake, though any woman with eyes would. Just because I find him irresistible doesn't mean you have to, does it?"

Eugenia was taken aback for a moment. Her sister had insinuated that Luke was handsome and that maybe Eugenia would like him, yet it was true that Lindsey had never really indicated that she'd done anything beyond enter them both in the contest. Eugenia suddenly realized that she had expanded the scenario herself to include a hoped-for romance, because Lindsey had talked so much about neither of the sisters being married.

Before she could comment, Lindsey continued. "All I did was enter you in a fabulous contest that had lots of excellent prizes. Why, the beauty make-over alone is worth a fortune! Of course, I think the look the stylists give you will be a fifties one, but it's guaranteed to be flexible enough to work for an improved eighties look after the frolic is over."

She shook her head. "Trust me, *I* wanted to win, but I was happy when you won. After all, as you pointed out, I do have excitement in my life. What do you have besides a classroom full of children and a bunch of old people at the nursing home?"

"Now wait a minute!" Eugenia protested. "My life's not *that* boring!"

Lindsey held up both hands. "I'm sorry," she said quickly. "That's not fair. It's just that I want you to be happy. I think this will be a great experience for you. Just tell me you said you'd go with him," Lindsey pleaded. "Please tell me that."

"All right. I said I'd go," Eugenia finally admitted, "but really, Lindsey, I'm not pleased about it."

"Pooh, you're just nervous," Lindsey insisted. "You'll do fine. You and I both know you need to get on with your life. I think this is a wonderful opportunity that literally fell into your lap."

"Tell me the truth," Eugenia said. "If you had won instead of me, would you be so eager?"

"Are you kidding?" Lindsey asked, brown eyes wide. "I'd be in heaven!" She laughed as she held up her hand. "Girl Scout's honor. I wouldn't be having all these doubts and doing all this complaining. The event's supposed to be fun, for heaven's sake! It's an honor to win! Personally I like Luke, but even if I didn't, I would still happily accept all the prizes. It's all so romantic!"

"Lin, you have romance on the brain."

"What woman hasn't?" Lindsey asked. "If you'd stop running long enough, romance might catch up with you. You're just shaky about this whole thing."

Eugenia settled back in her chair. Lindsey was right; part of her problem was that she was nervous; the other part definitely was Luke.

Suddenly Luke's big voice boomed from the radio. "Good morning, Eugenia Latrop! How are you today, pretty lady?"

Eugenia fought to contain the shivers that raced over her skin at the unexpected greeting. When she met her sister's gaze and saw that Lindsey's eyes were dancing with merriment, she quickly looked away.

"Yes, ladies and gentlemen," Luke continued, "Eugenia Latrop is the lucky lady who won the Fabulous Fifties Fun Frolic contest!"

He paused for effect. "We were discussing our plans last night—over a candlelight dinner. Mmm-hmm, do we have plans..." he murmured in a low, suggestive voice, "... for the party. We have the most wonderful plans."

He paused again, then said exuberantly, "Of course, all of you know that even though you didn't win the contest, you can still be a winner. This is a public party, and we have a selection of prizes that will delight every one of you."

He went on to list some of the prizes that would be given away to dance contest winners, and mentioned other contests that would be conducted during the three days.

"Eugenia Latrop and I are going to be there. Do yourself a favor and come join us in all the fun. And I do mean fun! If you can't join us for the entire weekend, get your tickets for at least one evening. She and I have things planned that you can't even imagine, so don't miss out!"

Eugenia felt a blush creep up her neck as the shivers were replaced by a rush of heat. "Darn him," she grumbled aloud. "Why is he making it sound so—so—?"

"So wonderful," Lindsey supplied. However, that wasn't the adjective Eugenia had been searching for. "It truly does sound wonderful, Eugenia," Lindsey said enthusiastically.

"Now listen up, Eugenia," Luke said, catching both women's attention and causing them to look at the radio. "This one's for you, honey. It's coming your way with my very best wishes and something else special from me."

"Honey!" Eugenia repeated irritably. "What does he think he's doing? He's really pressing his luck. I may change my mind yet and not do it!"

A romantic love song filled the room as Eugenia balled her hands into fists. "The sheer nerve of that man!" she cried. "He *is* trying to make it sound like some romantic interlude!"

Lindsey grinned. "Eugenia, that's just the man's personality. He's paying you a compliment. He said you were pretty. I think it's wonderful that he's so charming."

"Wonderful, indeed," Eugenia muttered. "He's egotistical! That's what he is. *All* he is."

Lindsey looked pensive. "I do wonder what he meant about something else special coming from him?"

"I don't know, and I don't think I care to know!" Eugenia declared. "You said it would be scandalous for him to become involved with the women who win. Well, even you can't deny that he's making this sound like something is already going on between us."

"Is it?" Lindsey asked, her brown eyes dancing.

"No!" Eugenia cried, her pulse suddenly racing as she thought of Luke squeezing her leg so familiarly in the car. Now why did that have to come to mind?

"Well, don't be so hard on him," Lindsey said. "You can't blame him for being a little egotistical. Believe me, women are waiting in line for him."

"I *do* believe you," Eugenia assured her sister. Wasn't that part of the problem?

She started when the doorbell rang. "I wonder who that could be?" she murmured as she looked at the kitchen clock. "It's not even nine yet."

Lindsey smiled as she crossed the room to the hall. "It's Brad. He's picking me up so you can have the car today."

"You shouldn't have had him do that," Eugenia said. "I really don't need the car."

When Lindsey opened the front door, Eugenia heard a cry of surprise. "Oh, they're beautiful!"

Still dressed in her nightgown, dying of curiosity, Eugenia was forced to wait until Lindsey had closed the front door to find out what was beautiful. Apparently it wasn't Brad.

"Look, Eugenia!" Lindsey exclaimed happily as she carried a dozen red roses into the kitchen. "I hope they're from Brad." She smiled. "I think I'm making a little progress with that man. He was especially attentive last night." She looked puzzled as she gazed at the roses. "But why didn't he bring them himself?"

"Read the card!" Eugenia cried excitedly. "The flowers are exquisite."

Lindsey set the bouquet on the table and tore the envelope from the pin that held it to a green ribbon. Both women eagerly leaned over the small white square as Lindsey started to open it. Lindsey saw the inscription on the envelope and drew her dark brows together.

"For the Lucky Winner," she murmured. She straightened up and handed the card to Eugenia, trying to conceal her disappointment.

"Lucky Winner," Eugenia said. "I guess they're from *him*."

Suddenly Lindsey laughed. "Yes, from *him*. He's right. You are lucky. Oh, how can you not be thrilled, Genia? They're so gorgeous."

"I could show a little more enthusiasm if they were from someone else," Eugenia announced, looking at the lovely roses. Actually she was a little flattered, and only Luke's arrogance helped her to keep things perfectly in perspective. The flowers smelled heavenly. She pulled the small card from the envelope and read it aloud.

Tonight's your lucky night, Eugenia! Meet me at Lincoln's Club for a nightcap. Eight o'clock sharp! Don't be late. I have something to discuss with you—more plans. Luke.

"Are you going?" Lindsey asked eagerly.

Eugenia immediately shook her head. "Are you serious? No way. I'm not at that man's beck and call. Despite what you said, am I wrong, or is he making the most of this contest to see me socially?"

Lindsey giggled. "I hope so. Maybe he does really find you attractive. Didn't I tell you that miniskirt of mine would do the trick? The rest of his audience should be so fortunate. I'm sure they'd kill to have this much attention from him."

"Well, let them kill," Eugenia insisted. "I'm not interested."

"Oh, go and see what he has to say, Eugenia. Maybe it really is Fabulous Fifties business."

Eugenia didn't know why on earth she felt a rush of disappointment at the thought.

"You'll have the car," Lindsey continued. "I'm going out with Brad again tonight. We were going to invite you, but this is much more exciting."

"That's a matter of opinion," Eugenia insisted, glancing again at the roses.

"You will go, won't you?" Lindsey asked. "Aren't you dying to hear what he has to say?"

"Absolutely not!" Eugenia insisted. Yet inside a tiny voice told her she *was* curious and, yes, she couldn't keep denying it, foolishly flattered. She couldn't help but wonder if Luke behaved this way with all the contest winners. Or was this treatment really something a little special?

She suppressed the silly thought. If it was special treatment, it was only because she'd hurt his ego by saying she didn't want to be his cohost. He'd admitted it was a first, and he'd be humiliated to have to confess to his audience that she couldn't come.

Feeling a little crestfallen, she told herself she could just imagine Luke pursuing her to prove a point, to show her that he could make her interested in him. She frowned, finding the implications of the thought frightening. She couldn't deny that he was physically attractive, regardless of how egotistical she found him. Wouldn't it be awful if she let her guard down—?

There was a sharp rap on the door that startled Eugenia from her thoughts.

"That's sure to be Brad," Lindsey said. "I'd introduce you if you were dressed. I'll see you late tonight. He's picking me up at work."

She started off, then looked back. "I really think you should meet with Luke. The better you know him before the party, the more comfortable you'll be."

Eugenia rolled her eyes. Could she ever be comfortable with that flirty, insufferable man?

"I'm not—"

Lindsey didn't wait for her to finish. Grabbing her purse, she raced to the front door as another knock sounded, this one more impatient. "Have fun with Luke," she called over her shoulder.

"I'm not—" Eugenia tried again, but Lindsey had already closed the door. "I'm not going with Luke," she said aloud, anyway.

She stared at the lovely red roses, then looked down at the small card. Lincoln's Club. Eugenia didn't even know where Lincoln's Club was, but she suspected it was on Highway 17. She glanced at the card again, then tossed it onto the table. She didn't care where the club was! She wasn't meeting Luke Newton!

Some time later, after she'd lingered over a sweet roll and several cups of coffee, Eugenia looked up when Luke mentioned her name again.

"It's time for me to sign off, ladies and gentlemen, and you, too, Eugenia Latrop. Don't forget our plans, honey. Now this is Luke Newton, your favorite deejay in the morning saying goodbye. Here's a kiss for all my special gals, and that includes you, Eugenia, and you too, Betsy and Jeanie."

As Luke made a kissing sound, Eugenia walked over and flipped off the radio. The nerve of that man! He'd included her with his other *special gals*. And for all the world to hear!

The more she thought about it, the more annoyed she became. Who did he think he was? The arrogant, insufferable thing! She reached for the phone and dialed the station's number, which she'd heard often enough to know.

"Luke Newton, please," she said to the woman who answered.

"I'm sorry. Luke just left," the woman replied. "Would you like to speak with Morris Gravely? He's on the air now."

"No, thank you," Eugenia said. "Could you give me Luke's home number?"

"I'm sorry. I can't do that. He's unlisted."

He would be, Eugenia thought to herself. He'd need to be for self-protection from all the women he made angry. Or, she admitted, from all the ones who were crazy about him. If Lindsey was right, they were legion.

"You could leave a message," the woman said pleasantly.

"Thank you, but no," Eugenia said. Then she replaced the phone.

Luke wasn't getting away with this. She supposed she would have to meet him tonight, if only to tell him she wouldn't tolerate him romancing her over the radio.

She was startled by her own choice of words. Was that what Luke was trying to do—romance her over the radio? No, she didn't think that was it. Maybe he carried on like that with every contest winner. Maybe he sent them all flowers and invited them to meet him, just as he'd arranged the dinner. The station probably paid for it all as part of the promotion!

Well, they had to reach some kind of understanding. She wasn't his regular contest winner. Even though she'd agreed to participate, he was going to have to stop embarrassing her on the air like that!

He would agree, or else—or else she'd tell him she'd changed her mind. That was what she'd do. Having decided, she put on her bathing suit and went to get some sun.

Lindsey lived in a quiet residential section, and Eugenia felt comfortable on the beach as she settled down on an oversize towel. Most of the tourists who flocked to the area stayed at the numerous motels and hotels on Ocean Boulevard. Even the teenagers cruising in their cars stayed farther down the boulevard, leaving this area uncongested.

Eugenia smoothed on suntan lotion, then glanced around at the other people playing in the water or stretched out on the sand. Although she'd promised Lindsey she would be sociable, she didn't really feel like it today. She wanted to be left alone with her thoughts of Luke. But only because she was so angry, she assured herself.

She saw what she assumed was a family, a mother and two little girls who were dressed in identical, white bikinis and tanned to a golden shade. The woman had on sunglasses, her only concession to the late summer sun's rays. She was a sexy beauty, her black hair caught up on her head in a fashionable knot.

Eugenia was reminded that she burned in no time at all; she had to hide behind lotion and under a hat. But then the beach wasn't her usual habitat. Clearly this family spent a lot of time sunning.

When one little girl happily called out, "Come and watch me, Mother," as she frolicked at the water's edge, Eugenia noticed that the woman nodded absently and kept turning the pages of a magazine.

"Just don't go too far into the water," she said, without looking up. "You either, Elizabeth."

Eugenia watched the children for a few minutes, then she rolled over onto her stomach and closed her eyes.

She awakened some time later to feel the sun beating down onto her back. Glancing at her watch, she was surprised to realize that she'd been sleeping almost an hour. She was fortunate to have awakened when she did, or she would have gotten a bad burn, for sure. She rolled over onto her back. She wanted to blame this on Luke Newton, too. After all, if she hadn't slept poorly last night, she wouldn't have fallen asleep on the beach!

Although a few more people had joined her, she didn't see the mother and the little girls anywhere. She pulled a book from her bag and began to read. She would stay only long enough to tan her front so that it would match her back. In seconds, she drifted off to sleep again in the hot sun.

With a groan, Eugenia got to her feet some time later, shook out the sandy towel in slow motion, then made her way back to the house. A look at her watch confirmed that she'd been lucky a second time. She'd only slept about forty minutes, but that was long enough. Feeling drugged from sleep and the hot sun, she returned to the house for a leisurely shower.

After the shower, she felt a hundred percent better. She dried her hair with the dryer, wishing that she had hair that didn't need curling. Most of the time she simply wore it parted in the middle and straight, but tonight she wanted curls.

She ate a sandwich for lunch, then puttered around the house, trying to decide what she would wear to meet Luke. The problem was that she didn't have anything she wanted to wear. She kept remembering the way Luke had looked at her in the miniskirt.

How would he feel when he saw her dressed as a *schoolteacher*? as Lindsey had said so despairingly. Well, she wasn't going to wear anything of Lindsey's again. She was going to be herself, and if Luke Newton didn't like it, that was just fine with her.

She didn't know why she was expending so much energy on a meeting with him, anyway. After all, it wouldn't take her long to tell him what was on her mind. She didn't care how she looked when she did it. Finally she settled on a short-sleeved, white blouse and a full skirt that fell to midcalf.

Having decided, she tried not to give it another thought, yet the truth of the matter was that she knew she did care what Luke thought. She also knew that no matter how much she assured herself that she was only going to talk to Luke about how annoyed she was with his "personal" radio messages, she was eager to see him again. The thought frightened her.

She attempted to occupy herself with a book, reminding herself how much she would savor the freedom to read until it was time to dress to meet Luke. But it wasn't easy. Luke kept intruding into her thoughts. Time dragged until finally she looked up the address for the club, wrote it down, and dressed for the evening.

As she studied herself in the mirror, she groaned again. In the skirt and blouse she *did* look like a schoolmarm! It was such a contrast to her clothing last night.

For months she'd hidden herself away in her classroom, concentrating on the children, trying to forget Daniel and the discomfort she'd experienced each time she explained to someone that she wasn't getting married.

With a start, she realized that she hadn't thought of Daniel a single time since she'd heard that she won the trip with Luke. But that was only yesterday, she reminded herself. It had been such a surprise to her, being the winner, allowing Luke and Lindsey to persuade her to take part.

It had all happened too swiftly. She felt out of control, as though she were being carried along by a swift current. She wasn't ready. Her stomach fluttered as if it had a thousand butterflies in it. Turning away from the mirror, she went to her bedroom and snatched up her purse before she could change her mind about going.

"If you don't go," she told herself aloud, "you'll hear your name on the radio tomorrow. This is the lesser of two evils."

All the way to the club, Eugenia tried to convince herself that she had to do this. The thought of seeing Luke again left her feeling oddly weak. She kept telling herself that her reaction was due to the fact that she really didn't want to see him, yet wasn't sure that was true at all.

She didn't know what it was. Hating the confused way she felt inside, vulnerable and churning with emotions, she slowed down and scanned the building across from her for an address number.

"Darn," she muttered.

She was going in the wrong direction! She turned around in a parking lot, then retraced her route. When she finally caught sight of Lincoln's Club, a smart, gray building in an exclusive section, she was fifteen minutes late.

An attendant parked the car for her. Eugenia nervously glanced down at her plain skirt and blouse as she walked to the entrance of the club. She should have dressed; she wouldn't have had to wear something as extreme as the mini, but she could have found something better than the blouse and skirt!

Well, it was too late now. She recalled how nice Luke had looked in his tailored suit last night. Apprehensively pushing up her glasses on her nose, she went into the darkened room.

The decor was beautifully done in shades of gray and burgundy. Eugenia heard the joyful sounds of laughter and merriment and the tinkling music of a piano. She decided that Luke was enamored of piano music. Perhaps he enjoyed the contrast after playing oldies hits each day.

"One for cocktails or dinner?" a smartly dressed young man asked, stepping up to Eugenia's side, a broad smile on his handsome face.

She glanced around nervously and resisted the urge to chew on her lower lip. She really didn't want to pick up that habit. "I'm supposed to be meeting someone," she informed the man. "Luke Newton. Do you know him?" This was one instance where she hoped someone did know the popular disc jockey.

"Yes. Right this way, please."

She followed him into another subtly lighted room, hoping that her eyes would adjust quickly so that she could see. It was still light outside and the contrast was startling.

She soon found that she saw all too well. The young man was leading her toward a table where Luke Newton, smartly attired in a white summer suit, was sitting with a brunette whose back was to Eugenia. Her cascade of long hair looked jet black in the darkened room. Eugenia could see one shapely leg, which was crossed over the other at the knee and very visible where the woman's dress parted. Four-inch, high-heeled sandals accented her sexiness. Neither of them had seen Eugenia. They were clearly involved in an intimate conversation; the woman was possessively clutching Luke's arm as she stressed some point.

Eugenia stopped dead. She was late, and clearly Luke hadn't bothered to wait for her. But then why should he? she asked herself. He had this beautiful, sexy creature to take her place.

She turned on her heel and retraced her steps. Her heart was beating fast and her pulse was racing. She felt unreasonably panicked; she realized that she was reliving the last time she'd been in a night spot like this.

Daniel had asked her to join him for a drink, and foolishly she'd thought that he wanted to talk about a reconciliation and a wedding date. She smiled bitterly to herself. She had gone, because it had been important to her to keep up some sort of facade with him after so many years.

And he *had* wanted to talk about a wedding date—his and someone else's! While he'd been engaged to Eugenia, he'd been seeing another woman. It had been her second humiliation, and in a way Eugenia couldn't explain even to herself, somehow more devastating than the first.

Even though she had known intellectually it was all for the best, because she would finally have to put Daniel out of her life, she'd been hurt all the same to think that he was blithely announcing his wedding plans to her. But then, after all, as he'd casually informed her, they were "friends" and he felt their newfound relationship entitled him to tell her his good news.

Her hand was on the front door when she heard her name spoken in that soft, yet commanding drawl.

"Eugenia."

She didn't stop or turn around. She wasn't ready for Luke Newton in her life. She wasn't ready at all. Let him make someone else his Fabulous Fifties hostess. She really didn't want any part of it. She didn't want any part of Luke Newton!

## Chapter Five

Luke watched as the tall blonde rushed out the door and let it slam behind her. "What the hell?" he muttered.

Why had she come, if she was going to run away when she saw him? He drew in a steadying breath and jerked the door open to pursue Eugenia. He wasn't really in the mood for another temperamental woman; it was the last thing he wanted tonight.

He'd just been arguing with his ex-wife about their daughters. The new man in her life wanted more of her time. Luke could accept that, and had in fact offered to take the girls full-time himself, but no, that wasn't what Joyce wanted, either. After all, she insisted, she was their mother. Luke knew what she really had in mind: she wanted him to take them on the spur of the moment, whenever her boyfriend wished to be free of them.

At least that was the way it seemed to him, but hell, maybe he didn't know what anybody wanted. He sure didn't know what Eugenia Latrop wanted. He hoped she was worth the trouble, because she sure was turning out to be a lot of it!

"Eugenia!"

She was restlessly pacing the sidewalk while she waited for the parking lot attendant to drive her car around. She glanced back over her shoulder, then ignored Luke.

Luke forced himself to smile and slow down. "Eugenia," he murmured when he reached her side, "why are you running off?"

"I didn't mean to interrupt," she said coolly. "Please go back to your friend. I wasn't planning to stay, anyway."

"She's not my—" Luke began, but Eugenia interrupted him.

"Really, I don't care what she is or isn't, Luke." Eugenia glanced away from him as she hurried on. "I just wanted to tell you to stop saying my name on the radio." Her eyes met his briefly. "It's embarrassing, and I don't like it."

He smiled faintly. Actually, it was just as well that she didn't want to hear about Joyce. He wasn't in the mood to talk about his problems with his ex-wife.

"It's a promotion, honey," he said softly in the sexy way that sent shivers over Eugenia's skin. "I need to say your name."

"And don't call me honey!" she demanded, the coolness in her blue eyes instantly replaced by fire. "I'm not your honey."

He chuckled as he studied her. "You know, I think I believe you. I seriously doubt that you're anyone's honey."

When he saw a wounded look in her big eyes before she turned her back to him, Luke put both hands on her shoulders so that she had to face him.

"Eugenia, come inside. Talk to me. You weren't interrupting anything. You were late. The woman came in unexpectedly, saw me sitting there all alone and literally seized the moment, as it were, to talk to me while I waited, but you and I had a date here."

"We didn't!" she countered. "You left a card asking me to meet you, but I never agreed. Besides," she murmured, "you obviously weren't pining away in there."

He grinned. "See what happens when you leave me at the mercy of other women?"

"I went in the wrong direction initially," Eugenia explained. "That's why I was late. At any rate, you didn't seem to be suffering without me."

His smile was fading fast. He had been suffering, and he didn't want any more. Did he want to deal with this difficult woman? He let his hazel eyes assess her again. He didn't know what it was about her that appealed to him so much, yet undeniably there was something.

Perhaps, he thought, it was because she seemed vulnerable tonight, despite the haughty demeanor. The contrast in her attire was extreme. The blouse and skirt made her look like a schoolmarm, as did her large, round glasses.

But maybe it was just his ego again. He hadn't been spurned like this often since he'd become Luke Newton, disc jockey. He didn't like it. He didn't like it one bit.

"Well, you came, so you must have agreed to the date," he said logically. "And I'm glad you came, late or not."

"I only came to ask you to stop using my name on the radio!" she insisted.

"Eugenia, Eugenia," he murmured, shaking his head. "Mentioning your name is part of my job. You won the contest and you did agree to go."

Eugenia looked at him helplessly as her teeth closed over her lower lip. "Luke, I—"

He wasn't being unreasonable, she knew. She was. She had agreed to go, and standing there beside him, her anger and panic ebbing, she suddenly felt foolish again, as she had felt when she'd sat at the table while Daniel told her his wedding plans.

Luke tilted her chin with one finger. "Please don't tell me you've changed your mind," he said softly. "We've been through all that. You gave me your word."

Eugenia swallowed hard and placed her hand on his to remove it. She couldn't think clearly when he touched her like that. It had been too long since she'd received a man's intimate attention, and she was acutely aware of this man.

Luke drew her fingers into his and she felt a rush of heat travel up her arm. "Come with me and let's have a drink," he coaxed gently. "Let's get to know each other, Eugenia—get to trust each other."

Suddenly he was feeling most peculiar; he realized how much he meant the words. He had been with other women since his divorce, but he sensed that this particular woman needed him. And that was important to him.

He felt that this, this flighty woman in her plain attire and big glasses was the real Eugenia. Her fingers were small and soft against his. He had an urge to tell her that everything was going to be all right, that he was going to see that she felt comfortable with him, that she had a good time. Yet that seemed a foolish thing to say.

He also wanted to shower her with attention, and maybe that was the best plan, he decided. Perhaps she needed to be shown that she was important to him, not just another female fan who'd won the contest. He smiled to himself: a contest she hadn't even entered or wanted to win. And she definitely wasn't a fan!

Her eyes were wide and very blue behind the glasses as they met his. The parking lot attendant drove up with her car. Luke waved the exasperated young man away as he steered Eugenia back into Lincoln's Club.

"Did you get the roses?" he asked.

Nodding, Eugenia murmured, "Thanks."

"Don't act so thrilled," Luke joked.

Eugenia stared at him. His handsome face was warm and open, his smile enchanting, his eyes questioning, as though he really did care about her reaction to the flowers.

She sighed. Why couldn't he at least be consistent? She could dislike him more easily if he was always like the man on the radio, but she didn't have much defense against this side of him. Keeping her distance from him demanded constant vigilance.

"The roses really were beautiful," she said.

He winked. "Good. A beautiful woman deserves beautiful flowers."

Eugenia concentrated on the door as Luke opened it for her. She didn't know how much of Luke's flattery and attention she could take before she succumbed. Like his other women, she reminded herself.

If she wasn't careful, she could fall for him hook, line and sinker. He definitely had charisma and winning ways when he wanted to employ them. She could think of a dozen clichés that would fit him. She was sure he could charm the proverbial birds right out of the trees. At the moment, she was as vulnerable and susceptible as any bird.

Eugenia had seen children in her classes with the same guileless innocence, but Luke's was only a front, she firmly told herself.

As he walked by her side, he commented, "I've never met a woman who didn't like roses."

There it was again, Eugenia thought crossly. She had been lumped with all his other women. She supposed it was inevitable with a man like Luke. First the sugar. Then the spice.

"They aren't my favorite," she said, some perverse little flare of defiance making her want to deflate his supersized ego.

"Oh?" He seemed surprised.

"No," she said casually. "Gardenias are." Actually, she was telling the truth.

Luke seemed to digest the information, but didn't comment on it. "Let's sit at the bar," he suggested. "Is that okay?"

"Yes."

She was relieved to see that the brunette had disappeared, yet felt foolish at such a reaction. She had come here only to demand that Luke stop using her name on the radio. She had done that, and he had explained that it wasn't possible. She understood. What now?

She shivered in response to the chills that raced over her when Luke took her arms and helped her up onto the tall stool.

"Are you cold?" he murmured solicitously. "The air conditioning is very efficient in here."

Eugenia smiled. "I'm fine." She looked at Luke, thinking how considerate it was of him to blame her response to him on the cool temperature.

Beware, she warned herself. The flattery inevitably came before the arrogance. It was so easy—and so dangerous—to like him when he was being attentive.

"Wine?" he asked, when the bartender stepped up in front of them.

"Yes, white wine, please," she said.

After Luke had ordered, he smiled at Eugenia, then gave his attention to the female piano player, who was running her long fingers smoothly over the ivory keys.

"You like classical piano music, don't you?" Eugenia asked.

Luke nodded. "I find it a nice contrast to the music I play every day. I believe it helps keep me stimulated and interested in all music."

Her eyes brightened. "I told myself that was the reason," she said.

He grinned at her. "Don't tell me you've been thinking about me, Eugenia!"

She looked at her wine as the bartender set the glass in front of her. "Perhaps a little," she admitted, tracing the rim of her glass with a fingertip.

"Well," Luke murmured, much too near her ear, "we're making some progress."

Eugenia took a sip of wine, then met his eyes. "Perhaps," she agreed.

He pretended to wipe his brow. "Whew, I can't tell you what a relief that is. I thought you were going to ruin my good reputation as a ladies' man."

Eugenia's soft laughter sparkled. "I don't think one woman has that much power."

He chuckled. "You might be surprised. A reputation is a fragile thing."

"Oh, I think Betsy and Jeanie would save yours," Eugenia said flippantly.

Luke's smile remained intact. "Do you think so?" he asked.

Eugenia took another sip of wine. She'd hoped he might offer some explanation about the two women, but then, what was there to say? His radio audience knew about them; he wasn't trying to keep them a secret. In fact, quite the opposite. He had openly said their names—right along with hers!

When she didn't comment, Luke sipped his Scotch and wondered if he should tell her that Betsy and Jeanie were five and six years old. The thought amused him a little.

Eugenia wasn't the first woman to wonder about his girls, but she was the first one he was tempted to tell so soon in the relationship. Whenever he did occasionally mention them, he deliberately didn't add that they were his children. It had saved him from an overly amorous female fan more than once.

"Do you know anything about a disc jockey's work?" he asked, resisting the urge to be frank with this woman.

Eugenia shook her head. "No. In fact, you're the first silver-tongued disc jockey I've met," she said. And with any luck, the last, she added to herself.

"Silver-tongued? Is that a compliment?" he asked, hazel eyes glowing.

Smiling self-mockingly, Eugenia shook her head at the irony. Luke would think it was a compliment.

When she didn't say yes or no, Luke said, "Well, you met Jordan Weaver, too. Have you forgotten him so soon?"

Eugenia shook her head. "Not at all. I found him quite nice." .

"Oh?" Luke murmured. He was pensive for a moment, then asked, "Would you like a tour of the radio

station? I'd be happy to show you around. I think you'd
find it interesting."

She nodded. She would like that. She enjoyed any
learning experience, and it would be something to file
away for the future when one of the schoolchildren told
her he or she wanted to grow up to be a disc jockey.

"That sounds interesting," she said.

Luke was pleased. He realized that he hadn't honestly
thought she would want to go; she seemed to dislike
everything about his work. But perhaps she merely disliked him. He found that thought infinitely worse.

"Good. We can go to the station tonight and you can
see Jordan Weaver work. Now *there*'s a ladies' man for
you! I should be so lucky as to have his night audience.
Women stay up until 1:00 a.m. just to listen to Jordan.
Have you heard him?"

Eugenia shook her head. "No, I haven't. The only
reason I listen to you is because Lindsey has the radio on
each morning when I get up."

"Oh."

Luke actually sounded disappointed, and Eugenia
wondered if he really cared whether she listened or not.
She was surprised that one woman would matter to him,
when he had such a fawning female audience.

"Not to worry," she added. "I'm sure you won't miss
one woman, and your audience must be every bit as vast
as Jordan's. Lindsey always listens to your show. I don't
think she tunes in to Jordan at night." She doubted that
Lindsey would change her habit now that they'd met
Jordan.

In fact, she herself wondered if Luke was joking about
Jordan being a ladies' man. He hardly seemed the type,
but unlike Lindsey, Eugenia didn't believe that attraction necessarily started from the outside. Jordan might

be a ladies' man. He hadn't hesitated to kiss both her and her sister's hand when he met them.

"At least one of you is interested," Luke said wryly. Too bad it was the wrong sister!

"Interested?" Eugenia murmured, having forgotten what they had been talking about when she started thinking about Jordan.

"I said at least one of you is interested in listening to me on the radio," Luke said, his tone bordering on exasperation. This woman really was hard on the ego!

"That's why I told you Lindsey should be the one cohosting the fifties party with you," Eugenia said.

Luke took her hand in his. "You aren't going to start that again, are you?" His eyes searched hers. "I want you by my side. You did agree. You can't go back on your word. You're not that kind of woman, are you?"

When his eyes held hers, Eugenia could really believe that he was serious. It was a dangerous belief, she knew, but she couldn't deny it, no matter how skilled and persuasive she suspected he was in these situations. She *wanted* to believe it!

"No, I'm not that kind," she murmured, even though she'd told herself a dozen times that she would change her mind if Luke didn't stop using her name on the radio.

Suddenly a petite, blond beauty walked up and wrapped an arm around Luke's waist. "Evening, Luke," she drawled.

"Good evening, Linda," he said warmly. "How are you?"

"Disappointed," she replied emphatically. "I wanted so much to win that contest. I entered dozens of times. I never win," she said with a sulky pout.

He grinned. "Keep trying, honey. I'd love to have you win."

He turned to Eugenia before she could let his words register. She felt tall and plain; she found herself wondering if Luke preferred short women. His words intruded on her thoughts with alarming clarity as he quickly made the introductions.

"Linda, this is Eugenia Latrop, this year's winner. Eugenia, this is Linda Ostermyer."

Linda energetically clasped Eugenia's hand in hers. "You luck thing, you!" she cried. "I couldn't talk you into letting me help Luke host the party, could I?"

Before Eugenia could comment, Luke laughed. "You know she couldn't do that even if she wanted to, Linda. It's not in her power."

He slid off the bar stool. "Now, if you'll excuse us, Eugenia and I have plans for the evening."

As he put his hands on her waist and helped her down, Eugenia looked at him in surprise. She was momentarily rendered speechless by the quick change in plans. She had not finished her wine, but that didn't seem important at the moment; Luke gave her a small squeeze before he freed her.

"Good night, Luke," Linda drawled with another sulky pout.

"Night," he said. "Tell the lady good-night," he murmured to Eugenia as he placed an arm around her shoulders.

Obediently she murmured, "Good night, Linda," then questioned why she'd obeyed Luke's command. She was letting him sweep her along in the current again; she knew she'd regret it.

When they stepped out onto the sidewalk, Eugenia pulled free of his warm touch. "I'll follow in my car."

"Nonsense," Luke declared. "I'll drive, then we'll come back for your car."

Eugenia wasn't about to stand for any more commands. "No," she insisted. "I don't want to leave Lindsey's car here. I'm going to drive."

Luke fought the urge to tell her he wanted her in his car, but sensed that she wasn't going to agree.

He smiled. "Fine. I'll ride with you. We can come back here and pick up *my* car."

Eugenia opened her mouth to protest, then closed it. Well, she'd gotten her way. What more did she want? Her eyes swept over Luke and she refused to let herself indulge in finding an answer to that question.

The man was much too warm, too near, too attentive tonight. He'd said he wanted them to get to know each other, to trust each other, yet she couldn't trust such a man. She knew better.

The attendant quickly arrived with the car and she slid behind the wheel, grateful to be occupied. After Luke had gotten in on the passenger side and moved much too near, he asked, "Do you know where the station is?"

She shook her head.

"You don't!" he chided. "I can't believe it, Eugenia. I've never been with a woman who cared less about me or my work."

She didn't know if he was teasing or not. She kept her eyes on the road as she drove off. "Where is it?"

After he'd given her directions, Luke turned on the radio, which was tuned to his station. "There's Jordan," he said.

Eugenia listened to the gravelly-voiced man announcing a song. She had to admit that she didn't find him nearly as seductive as Luke, no matter that he was on late at night and Luke had said Jordan was a ladies' man.

"Do you find his style more appealing than you do mine?" Luke asked unexpectedly.

Eugenia had to laugh. Could Luke read her thoughts? "I don't know. This is the first time I've heard him, and a few words about one song isn't much to go on."

"But you've met him," Luke said. "Now you've heard him. How about the voice?"

Eugenia glanced at him, then back at the road. "Oh, Luke, honestly, does it matter?"

He laughed, realizing that he sounded jealous of Jordan. Still, he couldn't deny that he wanted Eugenia to like him. That was what this trip to the station was about. He wanted this woman to know a little something about him and his work. He felt that if she understood, maybe—

Maybe what? He honestly didn't know why he was working so hard to get her to like him.

When they had parked in the nearly deserted lot of the station, Luke took Eugenia's hand again. She was sure her fingers were shaking, yet Luke didn't seem to notice. This time he couldn't attribute it to air conditioning; perhaps he'd decided being quiet was best.

He unlocked the door with a key, then ushered Eugenia inside the building. She really was enthusiastic about seeing the station. She quickened her steps as they made their way down the hall. Behind a glass window she could see Jordan as he talked and gestured animatedly, even though he was the only person in the room.

Luke found himself recalling that Eugenia had said she'd liked Jordan. Most women did, even though Jordan wasn't handsome. The joke was that Jordan really was the ladies' man; he had a way with women like no other man Luke had ever seen.

He dismissed the thought. He was well aware that women found him more attractive than Jordan. He didn't know why he was feeling insecure with Eugenia—perhaps because she was obviously so uninterested, he thought again.

After rapping on the window, Luke waved to Jordan, who grinned broadly and motioned for them to come in. Luke opened the door for Eugenia as Jordan put on some music and stood up.

"Welcome, competition!" the burly, auburn-haired man roared, moving forward to embrace Luke. Eugenia was surprised by the genuine affection and good-natured teasing between the two. She truly had expected them to be competitive.

"Jordan," Luke drawled, "you remember Eugenia Latrop—and, by the way—she *isn't* a fan of yours."

"Of course I remember," Jordan said, beaming at her. "I never forget a lovely woman." Then he frowned as he looked at an embarrassed Eugenia. "So you're not a fan?" He waved a hand dismissively. "Well, I suppose you must be loyal to Luke. He needs all the loyalty he can get, and after all, you're his contest winner."

For once, Luke didn't interrupt. For once, Eugenia wished he had.

"Yes," she murmured. "And, Mr. Weaver, I'm not a fan of yours, because I've never listened. I don't stay up late," she hastened to add.

"Well, bless you, dear lady. That's some consolation," Jordan said as he reached for Eugenia's hand and pressed it to his lips. "At least you're not completely prejudiced in Luke's favor," he said with a wink.

Eugenia was still trying to recover from the kiss when Luke spoke.

"How about not at all?" he drawled. "She's not a fan of mine, either."

Jordan looked puzzled. Eugenia was growing more embarrassed. She was beginning to regret coming here.

"Her sister entered her in the contest," Luke said, sounding appropriately rueful. "She's reluctant to even participate in our Fifties Frolic!"

Jordan laughed loudly. "Well, a first for Luke Newton! Rejection, once removed!"

"No fooling," Luke said, looking at Eugenia.

She made a vague gesture with her hand and shifted uncomfortably from foot to foot. "Listen, gentlemen, it's nothing personal," she said in a small voice.

"Nothing personal!" they both repeated boisterously.

Luke looked at Jordan. "What does the lady consider personal? We're here knocking ourselves out, no matter how we feel, and she's rejecting us and saying 'nothing personal'!"

Jordan laughed again. "This is one contest I don't envy you, Luke. I think you've got your work cut out for you." He gave Eugenia a quick appraisal, then turned back to Luke. "Obviously the pretty lady has better taste in men than to be pleased with you, buddy."

Eugenia felt her face flame. She really didn't consider herself pretty, and especially not tonight in the skirt and blouse. Oh, she realized that she was adequately attractive, but she didn't feel she lived up to Jordan's compliments.

"Thank you," she managed to murmur.

"For what?" Luke asked, pretending indignation. "Saying you're pretty? Or that you have better taste in men than to be pleased with me?"

As Eugenia felt her face grow hotter, abruptly Luke grinned and let her off the hook by turning to Jordan. "How's it going tonight?" he asked.

Jordan ran his fingers through his wavy hair. "I feel like going home and going to bed," he confessed frankly. "I did that promo with the bands earlier. My head is splitting, and I'd love to sleep twelve hours. Every sad song I play puts me on a downer."

Eugenia found his frankness eye-opening. She hadn't thought about how difficult it would be to play songs one wasn't in the mood for.

"Why do you play the sad ones?" she asked, intrigued.

Jordan grinned. "You don't know anything about the business, do you?"

Eugenia shook her head. "Nothing."

"We do our best to please the audience," Jordan explained. "We subscribe to a music service, which sends out tapes with the most popular picks and a cue sheet to follow. I push the right buttons to make it all happen. If I want to be innovative, I have to pull some old records or switch to backup tapes. On nights like tonight, it's a lot of work and energy I don't really have."

"But what about requests?" Eugenia asked, genuinely interested. She knew they played requests on this station.

Jordan smiled. "Love 'em!" he said. "We try to fulfill them all. We're happy people call in."

"Are you really?" she asked, doubtful. "Isn't that a lot of work?"

"Are you kidding?" he cried. "I love requests, especially when the ladies call!"

"Oh." Yes, of course. When the ladies call, Eugenia told herself.

The song ended, and she watched as Jordan quickly seated himself and pushed a button on the panel for a commercial. Eugenia listened as he extolled the virtues of water beds for a company on the prerecorded spot.

"Are commercials part of the job?" Eugenia asked Luke.

"Yes, usually," he answered. He smiled. "Actually, they're fun to do and most of us compete for them."

She gave her attention back to Jordan as he fulfilled a request in a low, warm voice, sounding very upbeat and enthusiastic. She hadn't thought about the disc jockeys having to perform, regardless of how they felt. Apparently they were like anyone else in the entertainment business; the show had to go on, whether they were up or not.

She smiled at Jordan when he came back, a sad song playing behind him. "Very professional," she complimented.

He laughed deeply. "That's what I get paid for." The smile left his face. "Seriously, I love my work. It's fun, it does pay well, but more than that, it's personally rewarding. I like to think I add to someone's night with music and input."

"Bravo! Well said!" Luke declared. "On that happy note, I'm taking my lady out of here before you win her over."

Jordan laughed as Luke waved, took Eugenia's arm and led her from the room.

Feeling slightly overwhelmed by the maneuver and the fact that Luke had called her his lady, she looked at him when they were again back in the hall. "I was learning a lot," she said. "Did we have to leave?"

Chuckling, Luke ushered her out the door. "I don't want you to learn too much from Jordan. You're welcome to come back anytime—when I'm on the air."

Although Eugenia didn't know how sincere he was, she hoped to take him up on the invitation. She really did find his work fascinating.

"I think it's time we called it a night," Luke said. "I have the 5:00 a.m. shift. Five comes very early."

"I'm sure it does," Eugenia agreed. She was ready to go home. Tonight hadn't been at all what she'd expected, and she needed to sort out her thoughts.

When they returned to Lincoln's Club, Luke started to get out of Lindsey's car, then looked back at Eugenia. "I have free tickets to the amusement park. Will you come with me tomorrow?"

"The amusement park?" she repeated.

"Yes. Have you been?"

"Once," she admitted. Was suave, man-about-town Luke Newton, famed disc jockey and ladies' man, really inviting her to an amusement park?

"But I wouldn't care to go, thank you," she added hastily.

"Nonsense," he said, completely dismissing her refusal. "You'll love it with me. I'll pick you up at six tomorrow night. Dress casually." Before Eugenia knew what he was doing, he bent forward and softly caressed her lips with his own.

Luke was gone before she could utter a single protest. She touched her mouth in wonder, put her car into gear and drove away. She had parked in Lindsey's driveway before she convinced herself that she'd have to tell Luke that he wasn't free to take such liberties with her. She had simply enjoyed the touch of his mouth too much to complain.

## Chapter Six

Her face suffused with color, Luke's kiss still warm on her lips, Eugenia hurried into the house. When she heard the radio on in the kitchen, she went there.

"What are you doing home so early?" she asked, seeing Lindsey slumped over a cup of coffee and a sweet roll.

Lindsey brushed some crumbs from her mouth and sighed dramatically. "Feeling sorry for myself," she answered.

"Why?"

Lindsey shrugged in resignation. "Same old thing, Eugenia. Every time I go out with Brad, I hope he'll propose. Once again I was disappointed." She pursed her lips and shook her head. "Oh, what am I going to do? There must be some way to get him to marry me!"

Eugenia patted her younger sister on the shoulder and sat down beside her. "I know one thing you'd better do."

"What?" Lindsey asked with such excitement in her brown eyes that Eugenia was sorry she'd said anything.

Eugenia made a rueful face. "I don't know how to get Brad to propose, Lindsey, but if you don't stop eating those pastries, you'll never fit in a wedding gown."

Lindsey waved a hand. "I'm frustrated. I have to do something to make myself feel better." Her eyes brightened again. "But enough of my misery. What about your evening? You met Luke, didn't you?"

Unconsciously chewing on her lower lip, Eugenia reached into the box of bakery goods and pulled out a glazed doughnut. She had taken a big bite of the delicious confection before she realized she'd done it.

"Look at this!" she cried, holding up the doughnut. "I'm starting to eat sweets like you do, Lindsey!"

Lindsey giggled. "You must be frustrated too, Sister. Didn't the evening with Luke go well?"

Looking away evasively, Eugenia nodded, then took another bite of the doughnut, chewed it and swallowed. She didn't want her sister to know how she'd run out of the night spot. Nor did she intend to confess that she'd let the disc jockey kiss her. Anyway, she wouldn't allow herself to make that mistake again.

She shrugged. "The evening was okay. He just told me more about the contest."

Lindsey held up a long-fingered hand. "Shh. Be quiet a minute," she murmured.

Curious, Eugenia listened. Jordan Weaver was saying her name!

"Yes, ladies and gentlemen," he continued, "I met Eugenia Latrop, the lucky winner of the contest with Luke Newton." He laughed. "Let me rephrase that. I met Eugenia Latrop, the winner of the contest. Lucky *Luke*!

What a pretty lady. I know they're going to have a fine time!''

The deejay paused and chuckled. "At least I sure know *I* would with that beauty. Now all of you will have a chance to meet her. Get your tickets as soon as possible to the Fabulous Fifties Fun Frolic. Remember we're only going to sell five hundred of them for the first and second night, and only three hundred for the third. I know I'll be there. I want to see more of Eugenia."

Eugenia groaned, shoved back her chair and raced over to flip the radio off. "See what you've gotten me into!" she exclaimed, looking back accusingly at her sister. "I'm tied to Luke Newton all over the radio! I hate being made so public like that! Good heavens, Lindsey! This isn't good for a grade school teacher's reputation!"

Lindsey dismissed her sister's outcry with a wave of her hand. "In this day and time, Eugenia, no one cares. Besides, you aren't even in the town where you teach."

"Hah!" Eugenia said. "You think no one's worried about reputations these days? Well, I'll tell you someone who is! Luke Newton."

Lindsey was clearly surprised. "Luke? I can't believe that. He seems to love being thought of as a ladies' man. Who told you he was worried?"

"As a matter of fact," Eugenia answered, "he did. Actually, he's worried that I'll ruin his bad reputation," she added wryly.

Lindsey's laughter was unrestrained. "That I can believe! You haven't exactly stroked his ego, have you? And now Jordan Weaver is in on the secret." She looked down at her long nails. "Boy, was I disappointed when I met him. Why couldn't he look like Luke?"

"I like him," Eugenia said. "He's really very nice. Luke took me to the radio station." She looked at the box of goodies. "I guess that was just for more hype. I should have known it was only so that Jordan could talk about the contest, too."

Lindsey shook her head. "I don't think so, Eugenia. I tell you, Luke's giving you special treatment, and Jordan's picked up on it."

Although Eugenia wanted to believe her sister's words, she wasn't that much of a fool. "You don't know that, Lindsey. I've never known you to listen to Jordan. It's probably part of his job to talk about the contest. If you hadn't been angry with Brad and I hadn't had your car, you wouldn't even be home now listening to him."

Giggling, Lindsey had to agree. "That's true. I've never listened to Jordan before."

"That's what I told Luke," Eugenia said. She laughed. "I think Luke's joking, but he insists Jordan Weaver is the *real* ladies' man."

"What prompted that?" Lindsey asked curiously.

Eugenia shrugged. "Luke appeared to want to be reassured that he was more popular than Jordan—or so it seemed to me," she murmured. "I told him you always listen to him, but never to Jordan. You made me out a liar tonight, of course."

Lindsey frowned thoughtfully. "As much as I hate to admit it, sister, you may be right about Luke. He may be leading you on. He's the most popular deejay on the air. I don't believe for a moment that he sees Jordan as competition. False modesty," she said with another airy wave of her hand. "Luke sounds better and he's better looking. I'm sure he knows it."

Although Eugenia had been thoroughly convinced herself, she was foolishly disappointed to hear Lindsey confirm her own fears.

"This is all so ridiculous!" she cried in exasperation. "Why don't you take my place with Luke? You're clearly enamored of him and you *want* all this publicity. Honestly, Lindsey, I don't like it one bit. I don't want to keep hearing about myself on the radio!"

Nor did she want to deal with Luke. Or Jordan. Or the contest. She really didn't. Just when she thought she was on firm ground, the rug was pulled out from under her. She couldn't take any more tumbles. This was getting more and more involved, and she didn't know how to extricate herself.

Luke had been absolutely right: she was afraid to be his cohost and be in the spotlight at the frolic. She wished she'd never heard of Luke Newton, notorious disc jockey and womanizer! She wasn't prepared to cope with the situation or with him. She didn't want to!

Lindsey studied Eugenia pensively for a moment after the outburst, as though she were considering her sister's suggestion. Leaving Eugenia in suspense, Lindsey savored another bite of her sweet roll.

"You'd still be hearing your name on the radio," she said at length. "The disc jockeys couldn't suddenly say it was Lindsey Latrop who won."

"No, they couldn't," Eugenia conceded.

She was surprised by the erratic beating of her heart as she watched her sister. She realized that she had been holding her breath in anticipation of Lindsey's response. Was Lindsey going to change her mind and go? And was that what Eugenia *really* wanted?

Or did she herself want to go with Luke now? It was true that she didn't like the publicity—but did she really want Lindsey to go in her place?

She was in turmoil; deep inside she suspected that she secretly harbored a desire to have the chance to get to know Luke Newton better. Pride had kept her from admitting that to her sister—or herself—until now. She knew how futile and foolish that desire was, but she couldn't forget the brief, tantalizing touch of Luke's mouth on hers.

She released her breath in a sigh when Lindsey shrugged off Eugenia's suggestion.

"That would never work," Lindsey declared. "It's too late, and I'm afraid it wouldn't have much impact on Brad. I should have listened to you to begin with. If Luke were showing me all the attention he's showing you, Brad would be jealous, I know. But it's all water under the bridge, anyway. I tell you, Luke wouldn't treat me the same way. I'm sure of it."

To Eugenia's chagrin, she wished that she believed that Lindsey knew what she was talking about. "He's just trying to prove that he can get me to like him," she said, verbalizing more of her fears. But Lindsey was too preoccupied to absorb Eugenia's comment.

"Eugenia, you've just got to help me come up with some strategy to get Brad to propose! You know how much I wanted a summer wedding. Summer's already waning."

Eugenia nodded. "We'll come up with something. Oh," she said, snapping her fingers, "by the way, Luke said he would let you participate in the frolic, if you want. That might help considerably with Brad, and truthfully, it'll make me feel better, too."

Lindsey squealed. "You're kidding! You mean I might get up on stage and the whole bit?"

"Sounds like it," Eugenia said.

"Hey, that's great!" Lindsey cried, reaching over to hug her sister. "Thank you."

"Thank *you*," Eugenia said.

She meant it. She was so relieved that her sister hadn't taken up her suggestion of taking her place as contest winner that she didn't know what to do. She picked up the glazed doughnut. Dismayed by the realization that she really wanted to be with Luke, she ate the rest of the pastry—and two more besides.

When Eugenia got up the next morning, she was sure she wouldn't be able to look at another sweet roll. All night long she'd had nightmares of being trapped in the hole of a gigantic doughnut. The only way she could get out was to eat her way to the other side. Her stomach still ached, and she never wanted to see another pastry as long as she lived.

"Oh, no!" she groaned when she went into the kitchen and discovered Lindsey in her usual chair, happily eating a jelly doughnut that had raspberry jam leaking out the bottom. Eugenia staggered to a chair and put her hands over her eyes.

"What's wrong?" Lindsey asked.

"I can't bear to look at another sweet roll," the blonde said with conviction. "I dreamed about them all night. It was awful!"

As she told her sister about the nightmare, Lindsey laughed delightedly. "That's not a nightmare! That's my idea of a delicious dream."

A husky, male voice boomed over the radio when the country song ended. "Good morning, Eugenia Latrop!"

"And *that*'s my idea of an even more delicious dream," Lindsey said. "I wish he was saying 'Good morning, Lindsey Latrop!' with all the gusto he puts into your greeting."

Eugenia caught her lower lip with her upper teeth, then immediately freed it. In spite of all her warnings to her-

self, she had gone and picked up Lindsey's habit. She was
just so frustrated by Luke Newton—frustrated and yes,
she had to admit, flattered in spite of being embarrassed
by all the hoopla. She wanted to hear what else he would
say, so when Lindsey continued to talk about Luke,
Eugenia was the one who made a shushing noise.

"Eugenia, honey, don't forget our special plans tonight," Luke said. Then he added with a husky laugh,
"Eat your heart out, Jordan Weaver."

An oldies hit with humorous lyrics began to play.
Eugenia didn't realize she was holding her breath until it
slipped out in a weary sigh.

*Was* she special to Luke, or was it all a part of the promotion game the disc jockeys were playing? She was beginning to feel like a pawn passed back and forth over the
airways for publicity purposes.

"What special plans for tonight?" Lindsey cried.
"You didn't tell me anything about tonight, Eugenia!"

Trying to dismiss it, Eugenia shrugged. "It's nothing
to get excited about, Lindsey. We're going to the amusement park."

Frowning, Lindsey wiped some of the dripping jelly off
her doughnut, then licked her fingers. "Amusement
park? You and Luke Newton are going to the amusement park? Did you dream that, Sister, or are you kidding me?"

The serious expression on Lindsey's face made Eugenia
recall her own disbelief when Luke had invited her. "I'm
telling the truth. Girl Scout's honor. It isn't exactly in
keeping with his image, is it?"

Lindsey giggled. "Huh! He'll find some way to work
it to his advantage. He'll probably have a camera crew
there to film the amazing event, so he can use it for publicity."

The mere thought made Eugenia cringe. "You don't think that's why he's invited me, do you?"

Lindsey laughed. "No, not really." She went to the sink and washed her sticky fingers. "Well, I've got to run. See you tonight before you leave."

Then, shaking her head, Lindsey made an abrupt decision. "No, I won't. Why should I come home and spend the evening alone while you're with that great-looking man? I'm going by Brad's office and taking him to dinner. Maybe I'll put a wedding ring in his wineglass."

"Lindsey!" Eugenia cried. "You wouldn't do that!"

Lindsey held up her hand. "Just kidding. At least I think I'm kidding," she amended. "I am getting desperate. I'm going to stop by and see if he wants to go out for pizza. I'll tell him I have a coupon."

"Do you?"

Lindsey grinned sheepishly. "I will have by the time I get there, if I have to stop by the pizza shop and buy one first."

Smiling faintly, Eugenia made up her mind that she really was going to work on some way to help Lindsey win Brad over, before her sister did something she would regret.

"Maybe we *should* have Jordan Weaver say your name on the air," she said distractedly, thinking aloud.

Lindsey picked up her purse, then turned and faced Eugenia. Her eyes were glowing mischievously and her features were animated. "You know what? You might have a good idea there. Jordan takes requests. I heard him last night."

Eugenia nodded, then wondered if she'd unleashed a monster with her words. "What kind of request are you planning?"

Lindsey shrugged. "I don't know. I'll think on it. Bye, Sister. Have fun tonight."

"I'll try. Good luck with Brad."

Lindsey winked. "I might not need luck. I'll see what I can come up with besides that." Her laughter lingered after she'd gone.

Eugenia wondered what was going to become of them both. Her sister was dying to make a marriage commitment, and she herself was afraid of any romantic involvement, much less a commitment. She sighed. Only time and fate would reveal the future.

Savoring her freedom, Eugenia ate a leisurely breakfast of cereal and fruit, nursed a cup of coffee and listened to Luke on the radio. She couldn't help getting excited when she heard his sexy voice. It was so easy for her to visualize the man, sensual and appealing in his tailored suits. She wondered what he would wear to the amusement park—surely not a suit!

The question caused her to speculate about her own clothing. After she'd searched through her wardrobe and decided on walking shorts and a matching blue top, she put on her bathing suit, picked up a wide-brimmed hat and went out onto the beach.

While she was laying her beach towel on the sand, she saw the same two little girls she'd seen yesterday. Dressed alike in tiny blue bikinis, the dark-haired girls were adorable.

Although Eugenia was tempted to go over and talk to them, when she saw they were with a different person from the woman she'd seen before, she changed her mind. The girl was young and obviously nervous about her charges. Eugenia didn't want to add to the young woman's responsibilities by turning up as a complete stranger and showing an interest in them. She would wait until their mother was there.

She pulled the book she'd nearly finished reading from her bag and worked her way into a comfortable position on the soft sand. After she had put the hat on to shade her eyes from the burning sun, she sighed contentedly.

Soon Eugenia was so totally absorbed in the classic about the Russian Revolution that she was transported from the beach to a snowy night in Moscow, complete with cold temperatures and chills. Oblivious to the world around her, she shivered as soldiers on tall steeds raised their swords and charged after terrified citizens fleeing down the streets of old Moscow.

Luke Newton drove by Lindsey's house en route to pick up his daughters. His ex-wife worked three days a week and left the girls with a sitter. Luke often took Betsy and Jeanie to lunch in nearby Surfside on the days Joyce worked. He drove slowly past the beach house, thinking that he would settle for even a glimpse of Eugenia, but he didn't see anyone.

More disappointed than he had any reason to be, he continued to Joyce's house, but found no one home there, either. He suspected the sitter and girls were out on the beach.

Searching for them, he spied a pretty woman some distance down the beach, lying on the sand, reading. Tall and shapely in a one-piece black suit, she was a vision to behold. Luke stroked his chin, wondering if possibly the woman was Eugenia. A hat and sunglasses completely obscured her hair and eyes, the two features that would be a dead giveaway for him, if he could see them.

He was undecided whether he should go over or not; before he could make up his mind, his little girls came racing across the sand, and his attention became focused on them.

"Daddy! Daddy!" two high, excited voices cried.

He waved to them and the sitter. His decision was made for him as he gathered up Betsy and Jeanie in his arms and started back to the house, so he could bathe them and change their clothes for lunch. He cast one last glance at the shapely woman as he left the beach. It was all for the best; even if the beauty was Eugenia, it was too soon to introduce her to his best gals. Much too soon.

Eugenia finished the paragraph before looking up to see whom the little girls down the beach were calling daddy in such animated voices. She never stopped reading in the middle of a paragraph unless it was an emergency. By the time she looked over her shoulder, she caught only a glimpse of the man carrying the children. He was dressed in blue jeans and a loose-fitting shirt. A baseball cap was pulled down on his head.

She turned back to her book and tried to lose herself in its magic again, but all she could think of was the man and his children. She could imagine the family unit—daddy, mother and two girls. That was the way it should be. Sighing, she tried harder to concentrate, but when she couldn't get interested in the story again, she returned to the house.

The hours seemed to drag by, no matter how she tried to entertain herself, but six o'clock finally arrived. Her hair left straight and parted in the middle, dressed in her matching outfit and white tennis shoes and socks, Eugenia waited impatiently for Luke to come to the door. She smiled as she recalled telling him she didn't want to go. Here she was, pacing the house, so eager for him to come!

And yet she still jumped when the doorbell rang. Making herself wait for the second ring, she tried to calm down. After all, this was Luke Newton, disc jockey, the man she had promised herself to keep at a distance. What was she doing, getting so excited about him?

"Hello," she said when she answered the door.

Luke smiled at her and let his gaze roam appreciatively over her tall frame. "Hello," he said in that sexy, Southern drawl of his. "You look ravishing."

Blushing at the compliment, Eugenia fought the urge to say the same thing about him. He wasn't in a suit tonight. He was dressed in attractive white slacks and a brown silk shirt that set off the brown in his hazel eyes.

"Thanks," she murmured. She indicated his clothing. "I thought you said casual clothes tonight."

Luke laughed. "I'm casual, and you look lovely."

"Maybe I should put on slacks," she mused.

"No way," he insisted. "I like you just the way you are! You're not about to deprive me of the sight of those pretty legs. I won't allow it."

Eugenia felt the color in her face deepen. She'd never had a man give her so many compliments; she found it very difficult to remember that he was a master at casual conversation and probably meant nothing at all by his careless comments.

She shrugged. "Then I'm ready when you are."

He grinned lazily. "You mean you aren't even going to invite me in?"

Eugenia really hadn't planned on it. She didn't want these outings with Luke to seem like real dates. She couldn't let herself get that involved. She didn't want to risk having Luke try to kiss her again.

"Lindsey isn't home," she murmured.

Luke chuckled in that deep voice of his. "So?" I'm over twenty-one and I believe you are, too. We don't need a chaperone, do we?"

Forcing a laugh, Eugenia shook her head. "No, of course not. However, you invited me to the amusement park, not an evening at home. I've been looking forward to this outing all day."

A gleam danced in Luke's eyes. "Have you really?"

She nodded. "Really."

"Fine. Let's go. You can invite me in when we get back."

Eugenia experienced another moment of discomfort, then dismissed it. Lindsey probably would be home when they returned. If so, she would invite Luke in. If not, she wouldn't.

After they got into the car, Luke reached back for something on the rear seat. He smiled as he handed her a single, perfectly formed, white gardenia.

"Your every wish is my command," he murmured. "I hope this pleases you better than the roses. Unfortunately, the florist only had one in an arrangement. I was afraid you wouldn't like the arrangement."

Eugenia was foolishly touched by the delicate white flower. There was a catch in her voice when she spoke. "Thanks, Luke."

"Here," he said, "I know just the place for this." He took the flower from her hand and slipped it behind her ear, nestling it into her hair. "Lovely," he murmured.

Eugenia wanted to look into a mirror and see, but merely touched the fragile flower. The sweet scent was delightful. She was more pleased than she should have been because of Luke's gesture.

When they reached the amusement park, Eugenia felt a small thrill of excitement. She had come once with

Lindsey, just to see the park. They hadn't ridden anything, nor had they eaten anything.

A thousand memories flooded her mind—memories of summer fairs and sights and sounds of childhood fun, as she and Lindsey explored fantasy worlds with their indulgent parents. Eugenia had loved the smell of freshly popped corn and the sight of cotton candy best of all. The mere thought caused sensations in her stomach, and she realized she was hungry.

"Have you had dinner?" Luke asked after they had gone into the park.

Glancing at him, Eugenia wondered if he really could read her mind.

"No. I don't usually eat until about now," she confessed, hoping it wouldn't sound as though she was asking him to buy her dinner.

"Good! I told you your luck had changed since you met me. I haven't eaten, either. What's it going to be? Ice cream? Cotton candy? Hot dogs? Candied apples?"

Eugenia laughed merrily. The park—and Luke's gift—had put her into a good mood. "Hot dogs first!" she cried. "Then cotton candy. Then ice cream—frozen yogurt in a waffle cone. I love it."

"It sounds to me like you love everything," Luke drawled. "Hot dogs, cotton candy, ice cream. Why not a candied apple?" he joked. "Are you hard to please?"

Eugenia's laughter sparkled. "No, I don't think so. I'll save the candy apple for later."

Luke caught her hand in his. "Eugenia."

She looked up at him as crowds passed by, suddenly oblivious to anyone else. When he said her name in that way, he momentarily captivated her. "Yes?"

"I can't let your first comment go by, honey," he murmured, his deep voice causing shivers over her skin, despite the warmth of the evening. As Eugenia gazed into his warm hazel eyes, he whispered, "If you're not hard to please, does that mean an old, broken-down deejay has a chance with you?"

Eugenia didn't know what to say. She wasn't prepared to answer his question. She still didn't quite trust him, and the fact that he had other women never left her mind. The thought was her salvation.

"You're joking, Luke," she said, a barely noticeable quaver in her voice. "The only reason you're a broken-down deejay is because all the women in your life have worn you out."

There was a tense pause, then Luke chuckled. "All the women? How do you know what women I have in my life, Eugenia? Tell me."

Freeing her hand from his, she started walking along with the other people moving toward the rides. "I think you know without me reminding you, Luke," she said, her laughter gone.

He clasped her hand again and drew her back to him. "Stop running away when I ask you something," he said in a low, firm tone. "I want to know what you think you know about other women in my life." He laced her fingers with his, making her a captive at his side.

Eugenia looked down at their hands. "I told you I do listen to the radio in the mornings," she replied flippantly. "You do remember Betsy and Jeanie, your two best gals?" she prompted.

Luke laughed as his eyes met hers. "What do you know about those two? Tell me, Eugenia."

"Really, Luke!" she cried, aggravated. "I think this conversation is pointless."

"I don't," he said. "In fact, I think you'd like Betsy and Jeanie. I'm sure they'd like you."

"This is nonsense, Luke!" she protested. "If you want to talk about Betsy and Jeanie, perhaps you should have brought them with you tonight."

His eyes twinkling with mischief, he nodded. "That's a fine idea. I'd love to have you meet them. Shall we go get them?"

"Absolutely not, Luke!" she sputtered, her voice cracking with indignation. He had such colossal nerve! "If you can't stay away from them for one evening, why don't you just take me home? *Then* you can bring them back and have a merry old time."

"Wouldn't you like to have a merry old time with us?" he murmured. The only hint that he was teasing was the light in his eyes, but Eugenia was too angry to notice.

"I have no intention of meeting them—or—or of being added to your harem!" she declared.

A slow smile spread across Luke's lips as he assessed Eugenia's outraged expression. He drew her closer to him, wrapping his free arm around her waist, his fingers still intertwined with hers. "Tonight is all yours. If you don't want those two along, then it's settled."

Pushing him away, Eugenia muttered, "Don't do me any favors, Luke Newton."

He quickly bent his head and stole a kiss before Eugenia could stop him. "I'm doing myself a favor, honey. Trust me."

"Two things I won't do, Luke Newton," she snapped, "is trust you and let you keep kissing me. And I've already told you to stop calling me honey!"

He chuckled. "So you did. Come on, sweetheart. Let's go get something to eat. I'm starving, and the sugar from those pretty lips only whetted my appetite."

"Luke," she said in a warning tone.

"Yes?" he asked, his expression pure innocence.

"Don't use *any* endearments, and don't kiss me again! Promise me, or I won't go anywhere with you."

Slowly shaking his head, Luke murmured, "I swear, Eugenia, you're one difficult lady to get along with. You're going to have to stop threatening me. You and I both know you don't mean it, anyway."

"Luke—"

Four teenage girls rushed up out of the groups of people passing by. "Luke Newton!" the oldest, who looked to be about seventeen, squealed excitedly. "Luke! I listen to you every day!"

She wrapped her arms around his neck and planted a kiss right on his mouth before Luke could escape her embrace. They rushed away just as rapidly as they had come up, giggling and twittering and jostling each other.

Luke gazed thoughtfully after them for a moment. He hadn't been prepared for the kiss; he tried to avoid such incidents whenever possible.

"Well," he said, glancing at Eugenia, "somebody wants my kisses. Now let's get some dinner."

Her breath escaping in a small sigh, Eugenia went with Luke to the hot dog stand. Yes, someone wanted his kisses—lots of someones—and wasn't that precisely the problem?

Eugenia watched the handsome disc jockey as he stepped up to the counter. The truth of the matter was that she did want Luke's kisses, but she had better sense than to indulge that desire. She would not be a number in his line.

"You want it all the way?" he asked, turning back to her. She was surprised to see that he was wearing glasses.

"I beg your pardon?" she murmured.

"Do you want your hot dog with the works—mustard, chili, onions, slaw?"

"You're wearing glasses," she said inanely.

He chuckled. "The rides dry out my contacts too much."

"Oh."

"About your hot dog? Do you want it all the way?"

She nodded. "All the way."

Maybe if she ate enough onions, she wouldn't be worrying about Luke's kisses. Maybe. But she seriously doubted it.

## Chapter Seven

Minutes later, Eugenia and Luke were sitting on a bench, drinking soda and eating hot dogs loaded with all the trimmings as they watched the passing parade of people.

"Delicious junk food," Luke said before he took another big bite of his hot dog. "Mmm."

Eugenia laughed. "Lindsey is the one who'd really appreciate this. She loves junk food. She lives on jelly doughnuts and coffee."

"You're not going to start pushing your sister at me again, are you?" Luke murmured, managing to look appropriately worried.

Recalling how afraid she was that Lindsey would take her up on the offer she'd made this morning, Eugenia shook her head. "No, just making conversation."

"Good." Luke reached out with his free hand and squeezed Eugenia's shoulder. "Not that I didn't think she was a lovely lady," he added, "but you've captivated me."

Eugenia took another bite of her hot dog, trying not to think of all the compliments Luke gave her. "Me and every other woman," she said after a moment.

Luke studied her for a while. What was it about this pretty blonde that made him want to bare his soul? He glanced around him furtively while Eugenia watched, wondering what he had in mind.

Abruptly he bent forward and whispered into her ear. "Confidentially, you've got me all wrong, but don't tell anyone else. I'm not the womanizer you imagine me to be."

"Oh, Luke!" she cried, exasperated, "no one would believe me if I told them that! You're a ladies' man, through and through. You thrive on all that attention."

He laughed, then realized that he couldn't deny part of it. He did thrive on the attention; he loved every minute of it. Still—still—if a certain, special someone...

"You're absolutely right," he conceded with a wink, "however, a man can change, you know."

Eugenia felt a sinking feeling deep inside. She'd foolishly hoped that Luke would contradict her observation. "A leopard can't change its spots," she said solemnly.

Chuckling, Luke wrapped an arm around her shoulders again and hugged her. "Then it's fortunate for both of us that I'm not a leopard, isn't it?"

When she didn't reply, he murmured, "You don't see me as a leopard, do you, Eugenia?"

She managed to smile. "No. I see you more as a sultan seeking to add to his harem."

"What an enchanting idea. I'll bet you'd look luscious in harem pants," he drawled playfully.

"No way!" she declared. "I've already told you I'm not going to be part of your harem. I mean that, Luke."

He squeezed her shoulder again. "Ah, come on, Eugenia. Be a sport. We could ride off on a magic carpet and make love above the clouds, where no one could see us."

She pulled herself free of his arm and stood up. The fantasy image was much too appealing. She could just imagine how wonderful it would be to make love to Luke. With or without the magic carpet.

"The only magic carpet we're going to ride on is right here at the amusement park," she declared. "Aren't you ready to have some fun?"

"I thought we were having fun," he murmured, his voice low and plaintive. "I know I was." He looked down at her hot dog. "Anyway, you haven't finished eating. If you don't eat as many onions as I have, you won't want to kiss me."

Eugenia sighed as her eyes searched his face, settled briefly on his well-defined lips, then met his gaze. He really was the most exasperating man. *And* the most appealing!

"I have no intention of kissing you, Luke."

"Again," he added.

"Again," she said dutifully, a shiver racing over her skin as she unavoidably recalled his quick kiss.

"Why? Didn't you like my kiss?" he murmured.

"Really, Luke!" she cried. "What will it take to get you to understand what no means?"

He stood up and took the remains of her hot dog. "A lot more convincing than you've been giving me."

Before she could reply, he threw the hot dogs into a nearby trash can and held out his hand to her. Ignoring it, Eugenia stepped up to his side, but Luke wasn't about to let her refuse his extended hand. Wrapping his fingers about hers, he led her to the merry-go-round.

"I love the sight and sound of the carousel," he said enthusiastically. "Want to ride?"

Eugenia watched the children atop the brightly painted horses. "Only youngsters are riding," she said unnecessarily.

"I can see that," Luke drawled. "Do you have something against children?"

The mere idea amused Eugenia. "Of course not! I adore them."

"Then you have something against oldsters on hobbyhorses?" he asked wryly.

Looking back at the gaily colored replica horses, Eugenia had to smile. She would love to ride. Although she had taken many children to parks and playgrounds, she hadn't climbed aboard painted horses in a long, long time.

The faces of the boys and girls on the carousel were happy and animated as they went around and around, up and down. There was nothing but smiles and laughter mingling with the ride's music, which had a bright, twinkling magic of its own.

"You're serious, aren't you?" Eugenia asked, meeting Luke's hazel eyes.

He nodded and grinned. "Cross my heart."

Secretly pleased, she shrugged at his choice of rides, and murmured, "Whatever." Then she quickly corrected herself. "Whatever rides you select are find with me. I love them all."

Luke smiled. "Do you really?"

She nodded. "Truthfully, I think it's great to keep the child alive in everyone." She smiled. "Working with children has taught me that. They're so open and honest and trusting. They aren't into game-playing,'' she said pointedly.

He agreed completely with her assessment. Jeanie and Betsy had taught him the very same things. After his divorce, his daughters had been the steadying force in his life. They still were.

When the world shook him up or put him down and he needed someone to care, his two little girls were there with unconditional love and devotion, offering him wet kisses and chubby-armed hugs.

Luke gazed at Eugenia for a moment, unaware that her last statement was directed at him. The more he learned about her, the more he liked her. He hadn't realized that subconsciously he'd delayed getting seriously involved with another woman because he had to be very careful, not only for his own heart's sake, but for the sake of his children, too. Jeanie and Betsy's lives would be affected by the woman he chose to love.

He drew in a sobering breath. Maybe he didn't have any choice about love, if the truth were known. He suspected that love found its own target—and that it had already found him.

Eugenia Latrop made his heart beat fast; she made old dreams and desires surface. And before all was said and done, he wanted to hear her say about him what she'd said about the rides. As foolish as it was this early in their relationship, he knew he wanted to hear her say she loved him.

"Why don't you have any children of your own?" he asked, before it even occurred to him what he was asking.

Eugenia's breath caught at the question. She hadn't expected it of Luke Newton. She wasn't about to explain about Daniel. Eugenia stared again at the young riders on the merry-go-round.

When she was a little more composed, she faced Luke. "Why don't you have any? Foolish question," she said before he could answer. "Luke Newton with children? Why, you barely have time for the ladies in your life, do you?"

That thought, too, upset her. She didn't want to entertain it. Suddenly she was acutely aware that her dreams were just as alive as ever, despite Daniel, and that hope lived on brightly in her heart. She still wanted it all—all the things a man like Luke Newton wouldn't want—marriage, children, a home. She hadn't become the carefree, contemporary young woman she wanted to tell herself she was.

And she was thinking of all those things again because of Luke! He stirred the embers of dreams and desires that still glowed in her mind and heart. She was a fool to even be here with him.

Seeing that the children were getting off the carousel, she seized the moment to get out of the sticky situation she found herself in.

"Come on, Luke. Let's ride!" she said energetically, the brooding expression on her features giving way to excitement.

Luke studied her for a moment. He'd been surprised when she turned the tables on him with her defensive question about children. He wanted to explore the situation further, but decided now was not the time. He had to be very careful not to rush this lady. He'd realized it all along. She had Handle with Care written all over her, and he could read very well.

"Fine," he said, taking her by the hand again.

When he'd given the tickets to the ticket-taker, the man said, "Children only on the horses. Adults sit on the benches."

Eugenia glanced at Luke, clearly unhappy. She really had wanted to recapture that childhood magic by climbing aboard a horse.

He winked at her as he led her to a large horse with an intricately carved face on the other side of the merry-go-round. Eugenia loved its brilliant blue and pink colors. She gasped when Luke abruptly placed both hands around her waist and lifted her up onto the magnificent carousel creature. His hands lingered warmly as he smiled at her.

"But the man said children only," she whispered.

Luke shrugged. "So today we're children. Are you comfortable, Eugenia?"

Her gaze meeting his, she could only nod and smile at his boldness. Suddenly she seemed to be caught in a time warp. All around her were the animated laughter and high chatter of children selecting their favorite steeds amid the gaiety of the carousel music, but it all appeared to take place very far from where she sat.

She couldn't look away from Luke. She felt warm and shivery at the same time. Her pulse raced. There was definitely a bond, a tie, something sparking between them as they gazed into each other's eyes, lost in this rare moment.

The ride started up and unexpectedly Eugenia's horse moved down. "Oh!" she murmured in surprise. She had been so engrossed in Luke that she hadn't been prepared for the movement of her steed. She reached out to steady herself, automatically placing her hands on Luke's hard shoulders instead of grasping the horse.

Inches away, he was still gazing into her eyes. "I won't let anything happen to you, Eugenia," he all but whispered in that husky, seductive voice of his. Then, as her horse moved up, Luke bent his head and kissed her lips.

"Luke!" she murmured, glancing around her.

No one seemed to pay any attention to the stolen kiss. All the children were absorbed in their mounts, smiling broadly, gazing out at happy parents who stood on the sidelines, watching with pleased expressions.

Eugenia's horse dipped again in imitation of a real ride, and when it came back up, she met Luke's eyes again. A second time he swiftly sampled her lips.

"Luke, stop," she whispered. "Get on a horse."

He looked into her eyes. "I can't," he whispered back. "They're all taken except the one on the other side."

Eugenia looked around quickly, then glanced back at Luke as her horse rose again. She fully expected him to try to steal another kiss, but he just grinned at her.

"I like the taste of onions," he murmured teasingly.

Eugenia rolled her eyes, wishing madly that she had some gum or mints in her shoulder bag. When she heard Luke's deep, soft laughter, she met his gaze again. Then she smiled.

"You had onions, too, mister," she pointed out.

He grinned winningly. "So I did. And you don't need to call me mister, lady. Everybody calls me Luke."

Her smile broadened. "I'm sure they do. And you don't need to call me—"

"A lady?" he finished for her. "Why, Eugenia, aren't you?" he asked, his tone teasing.

She laughed. "Why do you lead me into those dead ends, Luke? Yes, I'm a lady, but you don't have to call me lady."

"No? Then how about honey?"

"Oh, Luke!" she cried. "You really are impossible! I suspect you call all the women honey, just because you can't keep up with their names."

Luke chuckled. "Very perceptive, my dear Watson. You've found me out."

Her horse dipped again, and when she came up, she eased her hands off Luke's shoulders, turned her head away, and hung onto the barbershop-striped pole that supported her horse. Onions or no onions, she didn't want any more of Luke Newton's kisses. She was too vulnerable to his playful touch. She couldn't think straight when he caressed her lips with his, when he put his hands on her.

"Do you want to go again?" Luke asked.

Lost in thought, Eugenia frowned as her gaze was unavoidably drawn to his smiling lips. "What?"

"Do you want to ride the merry-go-around again?"

She shook her head. "No, thanks." She wanted to ride something where Luke couldn't touch her.

He grinned. "Then don't you think we should get off?"

Eugenia could feel the color creep up her neck. She hadn't realized the ride had stopped. The children were scampering away.

"I was just waiting for the kids to leave," she murmured.

"You wouldn't be hedging again, would you, Eugenia?" he asked. "I think you were off in la la land, daydreaming."

Although her first thought was a defensive one, when she looked at Luke's warm smile, she laughed. "You've found me out, Watson," she said, using Luke's phrase.

He chuckled as he tightened his hold on her waist and lifted her from the horse. For a moment he held her off the floor as he gazed into her eyes. "Tell me, sweetheart, were you daydreaming about me?"

"Absolutely not!" she retorted, but the betraying blush crept farther up her neck to her cheeks. "Now put me down, Luke Newton. I swear, you take such liberties with me!"

His laughter was warm, low and delicious. "You sound as old-fashioned as your name, Eugenia." He deliberately held her much too close as he set her on her feet. "Believe me, honey, I haven't taken nearly the liberties I want to take."

Eugenia's breasts had tightened at the slight contact with Luke's hard body and she didn't know whom to be angriest with—herself or him. She didn't recall anyone ever having such an effect upon her.

But then she hadn't had many boyfriends, and no one had ever teased her like Luke. Daniel certainly hadn't been the type.

"If you haven't learned that you can't have everything you want in life, it's time you did! Don't count on me being like your other women!" she sputtered angrily to cover her chagrin. The blush on her cheeks bloomed a bright red as she charged off the ride.

Luke easily caught up with her and drew her back by his side, an arm firmly around her waist. "Now hold on there, gal," he murmured. He tipped back her head with a thumb and forefinger. Eugenia's eyes were bright with rage. "Has anyone ever told you how beautiful you are when you blush?" he murmured low. "But then, you're always beautiful."

Brushing his hand away, Eugenia prayed she might get through this evening without losing control with this man. He had her emotions on a roller coaster, totally dependent on his whims and his words.

"Stop it, Luke. I swear I'll change my mind yet and not be your hostess, if you don't behave," she said severely. "If this is any indication of what you have in mind for the weekend, then you should state your intentions right now. I think you should know that I'm not that kind of woman."

"What kind of woman?" he questioned solemnly, eyes alive with mischief. "What kind of woman do you think I think you are?"

"Like all the rest you know!" she said sharply. "I declare, Luke, you are an arrogant, conceited man! Do you think every woman you touch is going to tumble for you?"

In truth, Luke was thinking how moments earlier she had included herself among his women. He wondered if she knew what she had implied.

He grinned. "I hope not. But then, I only touch special ones—like you."

"Enough!" she insisted. "I want your word right now that you'll stop these silly seduction tactics. Otherwise—"

Seeing that Eugenia was serious, Luke's smile faded. Jordan Weaver was right; Luke had his work cut out for himself with this woman. He'd never had anyone call his seduction silly.

Although he really was insulted, he didn't believe she meant what she was saying. She had responded to him, he knew, but she was still wary. There had to be some way to get to this woman without scaring her off in the process. He decided he'd better back off until he discovered how.

"You sure know how to dent a man's ego, Eugenia Latrop," he said solemnly. "Trust me, I won't inflict myself on you again. Even I can take a hint. And when a woman calls my loving silly seduction, that's hint enough for me."

When Eugenia met his eyes, she was afraid she really had wounded him. A woman did have to be crazy to call Luke's loving silly, but it had been the only way she could think of to protect herself from him.

"Luke," she murmured. "I—"

He smiled again. "I know. You want something else to eat. Fine. Let's have cotton candy, then I want to ride the roller coaster." When she appeared reluctant, he shook a finger at her. "You did say whatever rides I wanted to go on, didn't you?"

She nodded and fell into step beside him as he headed to the cotton candy stand. The roller coaster! It really did look intimidating, but she had agreed—

Three hours later, stuffed with hot dogs, cotton candy, popcorn, candy apples and yogurt, all of which had been spun, turned, churned and upended on a variety of rides from the roller coaster to the corkscrew, Eugenia was still laughing as Luke stopped in front of Lindsey's house.

"I had a wonderful time," she said happily. "Won't you come in?" She had forgotten all about her plan not to invite him in unless Lindsey was there. She didn't know there was anyone else in the world but Luke and herself.

Luke shook his head. "Thanks, but I believe I've had enough excitement for one day." Without another word, he climbed out of the car and walked around to the passenger side. He opened the door for Eugenia, then escorted her to the house.

"Good night," he murmured.

Reluctant to let the marvelous evening end, Eugenia repeated her invitation. "Sure you won't come in for coffee?"

Luke rubbed his flat stomach, drawing Eugenia's attention to that spot. "I'm stretched to capacity," he said.

She couldn't help but notice that the white slacks fitted him as flatteringly as they had when he arrived, but she didn't say that. Foolishly she lingered on the porch, waiting for him to say something else—waiting for him to do something else, she realized.

"See you later," he said, turning on his heel.

Eugenia gazed after him in disbelief. He hadn't wanted to come in. He had made no attempt whatsoever to give her a kiss, not even a little peck. He had been dead serious when he said he wouldn't "inflict" himself on her again? Did he mean he wouldn't see her until next Friday, the day the Fifties Fun Frolic started?

When he got into his car, it was clear to her that he wasn't kidding. He really was going—leaving—just like that. He hadn't said he would call or anything. Except that he would see her later.

Well, she'd gotten what she wanted. He was leaving her alone, as she'd ordered him to. She opened the front door, then stepped into the hall.

"Darn it!" she muttered.

Luke had done what she asked, and now she wasn't sure that she was pleased about it. She had an empty feeling inside as she went to her room. She didn't know what she wanted anymore!

Taking the wilted gardenia from her hair, she gazed at it thoughtfully. Its sweet scent lingered provocatively, but the petals had been crushed and withered by wind and rides and lack of nourishment.

If she wasn't very careful, Eugenia told herself solemnly, she would end up like the flower—stolen from her safe, secure haven, exposed to Luke's charm and charisma, battered and bruised by his reckless seduction—and left with only the sweet memory when it was all over.

She couldn't let that happen. She wouldn't!

## Chapter Eight

Eugenia jumped when she heard a rap on her bedroom door. She whirled and opened it, to find Lindsey looking distressed, despite the sweet roll she was munching.

"I didn't even know you were home. What's wrong?" she asked.

Lindsey sighed dramatically. "The pizza didn't work. Eugenia, what am I going to do? I've just got to get Brad to propose. I swear I'm going to *die* an old maid at this rate."

Glad to have something to think about beside her own problems, Eugenia laughed. "I guess you haven't heard that no woman dies an old maid anymore, nor have you heard that women are getting married later and later."

"Other women may be!" Lindsey declared. "I, myself, am falling behind in my life's goal! I swear I thought I'd be married to a handsome, wealthy man by the time I was twenty-one! With every passing year, I begin to lose a little more hope, and two have passed since I was

twenty-one. The next thing I know, it'll be fat thighs and
gray hair for me, and the rich men will be chasing the
young girls!''

Eugenia laughed so hard that her sides hurt. Finally
she nodded. "You may be right about the fat thighs.
Look at you eating that sweet roll!''

"A girl has to have some satisfaction in life," Lindsey
said, so solemnly that Eugenia laughed again.

"Genia, it's not funny!" Lindsey declared tartly, her
dark eyes flashing. "Time's wasting for me, and Brad's
not even hinting at a proposal. I'm just going to have to
give up on him, if he doesn't do something soon.''

"What did he say when you arrived with the pizza
coupon?'' Eugenia asked.

Lindsey shrugged. "He said the pizza sounded delicious. We went to the pizza shop, ate the pizza, and then
guess what happened?''

"What?''

"I came home," Lindsey said, sounding deflated.

"Where did Brad go?'' Eugenia asked.

"Home, I hope,'' Lindsey replied, looking alarmed.

Her fair brows meeting in a frown, Eugenia asked,
"What does he do at night when he's not with you?''

"How do I know?'' Lindsey cried. "And, no thank
you, I don't care to even speculate, if that's what you
mean.''

Eugenia smiled. "Actually, I wondered if he listened
to the radio. You know we talked about you making a
special request on the air with Jordan.''

"You know, that might work! I think he listens to
Jordan,'' Lindsey said. "In fact, I know he likes to fall
asleep listening to music, and I know he doesn't listen to
country or rock. He says the old songs are relaxing after
working with figures all day.''

"Figures?" Eugenia repeated.

Both women laughed.

"Numbers," Lindsey corrected herself. "At least it had better be numbers. I'm afraid that's part of the problem. Rich men think about numbers too much: stock, land, buy, sell, business. They forget about romance, when money dances in their heads."

"Well, get on the phone, call Jordan and make a special request," Eugenia suggested. "You can fib a bit and make up another man. Just don't give a last name. If Brad is listening, at least it might wake him up a little."

"You know, that's not a half-bad idea," Lindsey said, heading for the phone. She stopped suddenly, almost crashing into Eugenia, who was following her, eager to hear what her sister would say.

"Speaking of deejays," Lindsey said, "in my misery, I forgot to even ask about your date with Luke at the amusement park. How was it?"

"Okay," Eugenia replied, thinking what an understatement that was. "Hurry up and call!" she said, changing the subject back to Jordan as quickly as possible. She didn't want to talk about Luke. "I want to hear what you're going to say," she continued excitedly. She was soon dying of curiosity as she listened to Lindsey's end of the conversation, which lasted through three entire records, with Lindsey giggling intermittently.

"What happened?" Eugenia asked when her sister finally put the phone down.

"Just listen and you'll see," Lindsey responded, her brown eyes full of mischief. "You know, Genia, I think you're right about Jordan. He's very, very nice."

"Oh?" Eugenia murmured. "You didn't seem to think so when you met him."

Lindsey didn't seem fazed at all by the comment. "He said I was lovely, and he simply had to see me again," she murmured.

Eugenia shrugged. "You act as if that's a first for you. I happen to know that it occurs frequently."

"But not with Jordan," Lindsey said, the expression in her eyes dreamy.

Snapping her fingers, Eugenia said, "Lin! Wake up. I think you must be sleeping. This isn't your dream man! Jordan Weaver is a stocky, redheaded, probably poor disc jockey."

"I know," Lindsey murmured, as though mesmerized.

Abruptly the music ended, and Jordan's gravelly voice came onto the air. "Well, friends, I've had my thrill for the night," he said in a sensuous, low voice. "Our contest winner Eugenia Latrop's pretty sister just called to make a request. Boy, did it ever cause my heart to pound. She's just as beautiful as Eugenia is, and, fans, she's going to be at the Fifties Fun Frolic each night, so if you want a thrill, come on out and meet these beauties."

He paused, then added, "All right, you pretty thing, Lindsey, this is for you and—and—Oh, gosh, I forgot what you said his name was, so this is for you and me. Happy listening!"

While Eugenia tried to digest it all, Lindsey laughed delightedly. "Isn't he grand? Brad will pop a cork when he hears! I hope he eats his heart out with jealousy!"

She barely caught her breath. "And not only that, Eugenia! You, Luke, Jordan and I are going out to dinner tomorrow night."

"Hey!" Eugenia held up both hands. "Now wait a minute. Luke hasn't said anything about that, and I certainly haven't said I'd go."

"You *must*!" Lindsey cried. "It's more business for the frolic, and Jordan is going to arrange to have photographers there."

Eugenia shook her head. "You go with Jordan. I'm not about to go, unless Luke himself issues the invitation."

"Genia, you're doing it again," Lindsey said. "You seem to forget that you did agree to cohost this thing. Now you're trying to ruin any part I may play in it. Stop being such a meanie! Think about me for a change."

"Oh, Lord," Eugenia muttered. "Lindsey, you can try to lay a guilt trip like no one I've ever seen. You're better at it than Mother. I *will* not go unless Luke calls me himself, and I mean it."

A pout on her lips, Lindsey put her half-finished doughnut back into the box. "Thanks a lot!" she muttered. "I'm going to bed. Maybe by tomorrow you'll be more fair about this."

"Maybe," Eugenia responded, just as angry as her younger sister, "but I seriously doubt it."

Eugenia marched down the hall to her room, her head held high. When she was out of sight, Lindsey reached for the telephone again.

Eugenia was still sulking the next morning when she went into the kitchen, where Lindsey was indulging in her inevitable sweet rolls and hot coffee. The truth of the matter was that Eugenia wanted very much to go with Luke, Lindsey and Jordan tonight.

She knew she was way too eager to see Luke, to spend time with him alone, but Lindsey and Jordan, whom Eugenia already liked, would make a perfect foursome. Still, pride forbade her to go.

"Good morning," Lindsey said cheerily. "I hope you're feeling better this morning."

Too proud to let even Lindsey know how much last night had mattered to her, Eugenia said, "Yes, thank you. I slept well and I feel fine." Both lies, she told herself.

"Great!" Lindsey said enthusiastically. "Then you'll go tonight! What are you planning to wear?"

Sighing, Eugenia did her best to control her anger. "I'm not planning to wear anything."

"Oh!" Lindsey squealed. "I suspect Luke and Jordan both might like that, but don't you think it's a tad tacky for a prim and proper schoolteacher?"

Eugenia couldn't keep from laughing. Lindsey had always been able to make her older sister laugh, just when she wanted most not to.

"You are truly incorrigible," Eugenia said.

Lindsey giggled. "I certainly hope so. Now, truthfully, what are you wearing? I think I'll wear that white pantsuit of mine. It sets off my dark hair and shows my figure to advantage, don't you think?"

"Yes, in fact I do," Eugenia replied, recalling the sexy suit, "but who merits the 'knock-'em-out' outfit? Luke?"

Waving a hand airily, Lindsey said, "Of course not." Her dark eyes sparkled. "I just can't bear to disappoint Jordan. You should have heard the compliments he was giving me last night when I talked to him. Golly, it's so much nicer to have a man chasing you than vice versa."

"Chasing you?" Eugenia asked, surprised that Jordan was even in the running. "Now, Lindsey, you aren't going to play with that poor man just to make Brad jealous, are you? Luke's one thing, but Jordan doesn't deserve being treated like a puppet on a string."

Lindsey laughed again. "Tell you what, big sister. I think Jordan Weaver can take care of himself. You worry too much! I swear, I wish I was the man-killer you think I am."

"But Jordan's not rich *or* handsome," Eugenia pointed out.

"No," Lindsey replied thoughtfully. "Still, though, there's something about him." She shrugged. "Oh, I don't know what it is. Anyway, it's just through the frolic. I don't intend to marry the man, for heaven's sake. Now, for the last time, what are you going to wear?"

A stubborn expression entered Eugenia's blue eyes. "For the last time, I'm not going."

"Eugenia!" Lindsey cried in sheer exasperation. "You *are* going to wind up an old maid! I swear, you're so inflexible! If I can go help get the weekend arranged, you as the *winner* certainly can put yourself out for one evening."

"You got an invitation. I didn't," Eugenia maintained obstinately, her chin thrust forward.

At just that moment, as though planned, Luke's sexy voice filled the room. "Don't forget our plans for tonight, Eugenia," he said. "Oh, but I do *love* our plans. Listen, friends, we have a to-do planned for Labor Day weekend like you've never imagined. Now get your tickets while they last. They're going fast. And Eugenia, see you at seven o'clock tonight. Okay?"

Her brown eyes sparkling, Lindsey met Eugenia's surprised expression. "Are you happy now? There's your invitation."

Eugenia drew in a steadying breath and exhaled slowly. "It's not exactly an invitation, but I guess since it's business I can be—what did you call it?—flexible."

"Good girl," Lindsey said, finishing off the last of her sweet roll. "Have some breakfast. I've got to run. See you at six tonight, and Genia, you might want to look in my closet for something to wear."

"Thanks, but no thanks," Eugenia said, knowing her sister meant well. Still, she didn't know what she was going to wear.

To her chagrin, she realized that she was considering going shopping for clothes for an evening with Luke to which she'd only received the most casual of invitations.

She sighed. What could she do? She wanted to go. And she wanted to look good.

By six that night, Eugenia was just stepping out of the shower as Lindsey rushed into the house.

"I've got to hurry," she called out, so loudly that Eugenia could have heard her from anywhere in the house. "I want to look especially nice. Would you believe Brad *did* hear the request last night, and he called me at work!"

Lindsey's laughter echoed as she stripped off her clothes en route to her turn in the shower.

Eugenia was glad she'd already finished bathing. She, too, wanted to look especially good tonight, and was eager to see what Lindsey thought of her new turquoise jumpsuit. The material was sleek and clingy. Eugenia had bought matching three-inch-heeled sandals. Basically all there was to the shoes was a wide strap with turquoise stones; they and the jumpsuit made a rather daring ensemble for her.

She'd decided to curl her hair, but still gather it into a clasp at the back of her neck. She set about dressing, while Lindsey did the same. At exactly ten minutes to seven, both sisters entered the living room.

"You look so *classy*!" Lindsey cried. "My word, Eugenia! I think you may shed your staid image yet! That outfit is *really* divine!"

Eugenia could feel the color suffuse her cheeks. She felt that she looked good, and relished the feeling. "I'm no match for you in that stunning white suit, but I hope I'll do."

"You'll do just fine." Lindsey eyed her sister's clasped hair critically. "I think a French braid might be better, however. You need your hair away from your face, but that clasp looks old-fashioned."

Eugenia didn't want to change too drastically or too rapidly. She had to feel at home with herself. The doorbell suddenly rang and she nearly jumped out of her skin.

"Well, it's too late now," Lindsey said. "They're here. Next time we'll work on the hair."

Next time? Eugenia thought. She didn't know if she could get through this time. Her stomach was suddenly churning and she was more nervous than she'd been in a long, long time.

Lindsey's voice rang with enthusiasm as she said, "Do come in!"

Trying not to devour her lower lip, Eugenia waited anxiously to see what Luke would say when he saw her. She bit down harder when only Jordan came into the living room.

"Hello, Eugenia," he said warmly. "My, but you two ladies look spectacular! Am I one lucky man tonight! Let's get going, so I can show you off!"

Her heart sinking like a stone, Eugenia was dying to know why Luke wasn't here, but had too much pride to ask. Damn the man! He had *her* jumping around like a puppet on a string!

She was grateful when Lindsey asked, "What happened to Luke?"

Jordan laughed. "I wouldn't let him come."

"What do you mean, you wouldn't let him come?" Lindsey demanded.

Jordan chuckled. "I'm teasing. He's running late tonight. We're meeting him at the restaurant."

Eugenia was shocked by the rush of relief that sped through her. At least he was showing up. She had never imagined she would get to this point with that impossible man, but here she was, nevertheless.

Bless Jordan, he took both their hands and escorted them to his car, making Eugenia feel as comfortable with him as if he really were her escort, too. In minutes they had arrived at an exclusive restaurant right on the beach. Eugenia's heart sank again as the hostess led them to a reserved table. Luke wasn't there!

"Let's have a drink," Jordan suggested affably. "I'm sure Luke will be along soon. He never misses a meal."

"I'll bet you don't, either," Lindsey told him, causing Eugenia to suck in her breath in surprise. Although Eugenia was afraid Jordan would be insulted, he laughed heartily.

"You've got that right, pretty woman. I have a big appetite for all of life, and that includes food, fun and fabulous ladies." He draped an arm around Lindsey's chair. "Besides," he murmured, "this way, there's more of me to love."

Both of them laughed. Relieved because Jordan wasn't upset, Eugenia laughed, too. Soon they were all drinking wine and talking about where they had grown up. Jordan had spent his childhood in Roanoke, Virginia. They rapidly discovered that they had a lot in common.

By the time Luke arrived, Eugenia was laughing too hard at Jordan's jokes to be nervous or upset, despite seeing how handsome and suave Luke looked in a navy-blue suit that did incredible things for his lean waist and broad shoulders. A ruffled, white silk shirt complemented the outfit and, oddly enough, made the man wearing it appear even more masculine.

Eugenia told herself that Luke Newton looked like a male model tonight; every hair was in place, every article of clothing precisely designed to catch the observer's eye. She felt like a fool, but she couldn't stop staring at him. Every time she saw him, he was more appealing.

"Good evening," he said smoothly, seating himself next to her. "I'm sorry I'm late. Female problems."

He and Jordan laughed. In truth, Luke's ex-wife Joyce had dropped by at the last moment, claiming the new man in her life had invited her away for a few days, so she just had to leave Betsy and Jeanie with him right then.

He had searched frantically for a suitable baby-sitter, which had been a difficult task on the spur of the moment. He didn't want to miss the dinner *or* cause his children to feel abandoned. He had to take time to get them settled in with the sitter.

When Luke caught the strained expression on Eugenia's face, he opened the small box he was carrying and produced a fragrant gardenia. "I hope this makes up for the delay," he murmured.

Damn him, Eugenia told herself. With Luke she never knew whether to be angry or thrilled.

"Thank you," she said simply.

Her eyes widened when he leaned over and unclasped her hair, running his fingers through it to loosen it. Then he used the clasp to pin back one side behind her ear before he secured the gardenia there.

"By the way," he whispered, "you look beautiful."

Eugenia blushed and glanced at Jordan and Lindsey, but they were too engrossed in laughter to hear what Luke had said.

"Thank you," Eugenia murmured again. "So do you."

Luke's eyes sparkled. "Do you really think I look beautiful?"

Eugenia's face turned redder. "You look nice."

"Thanks," Luke said with an easy grin. "I went out and bought this suit today, just for you."

"Did you really?" she asked, sure he was teasing.

He nodded. "I did—really."

She smiled. "And I went out and bought this, just for you."

He laughed. "Too bad we didn't shop in the same place. We could have had lunch."

"Yes," she agreed, the idea thrilling her unreasonably. Somewhere between the last time she'd seen Luke and now, she seemed to have completely abandoned her determination to keep her distance from him. Even now, all she could think of was his kisses when she rode the carousel at the amusement park. Fortunately he seemed to have forgotten his vow not to "inflict" himself on her.

A waiter appeared and Luke ordered a drink. As the man turned away, a photographer, laden with camera equipment of every kind, came to the table.

"Before you start to eat, Luke," the young man said, "let's get some shots."

"Great idea!" Luke said enthusiastically. "We definitely must do it before dinner. I don't want Jordan having spots on his tie from his meal."

Everyone laughed good-naturedly. "Your day will come, Luke," Jordan said. "Mr. Bandbox will one day

dribble something icky down the front of him. It's life.
It's inevitable. It's destiny. It's the fate of the man in the
public eye!"

Luke shook his head. "Not in your lifetime, Jordan. I
wouldn't give you the satisfaction of seeing it happen to
me."

Jordan retaliated with a patient reply. "We'll see,
Newton. We'll see. Even you can't change destiny! By the
way," he said, turning to Eugenia and Lindsey, "this is
Jonsey."

The young man, already busy deciding upon the best
poses, nodded. "First, let's have you and the contest
winner stand," he suggested to Luke. "Which lady is it?"

Luke slid back Eugenia's chair. "This is the lucky gal,"
he teased.

For the first time, Eugenia didn't resent his playful
conceit. She did indeed feel lucky; that made her nervous, but not nearly as much as when Luke put an arm
around her waist and drew her close.

"Mmm, you smell wonderful, too," he whispered.

"It's the gardenia," Eugenia murmured, a little embarrassed.

Luke shook his head and briefly nuzzled her neck.
"Nope. It's perfume."

Eugenia felt the blush all the way to the tips of her toes,
especially when the photographer took advantage of the
moment to take a picture.

"Luke!" she protested. "He's not going to use that
photo, is he?"

Luke laughed. "No. I'll keep that one for myself."

Eugenia was only a little mollified when the photographer took several more shots before asking Jordan and
Lindsey to join Luke and Eugenia. The waiter had returned with a drink for Luke. The photographer sug-

gested they toast Eugenia first, then that all four of them toast the success of the Fabulous Fifties Fun Frolic.

All went well when Luke, Jordan and Lindsey toasted Eugenia, but when Eugenia lifted her wineglass to touch the other three, Luke suddenly drew her nearer, his arm tight around her waist.

The unexpected movement caused Eugenia to lose her grasp on her wineglass. The liquid sloshed out as though divinely directed and landed right on Luke's white, ruffled shirt. The stain spread rapidly, running nearly the length of the front of the garment.

Jordan howled with laughter and the photographer kept right on shooting, while Eugenia looked stricken, Lindsey tried to contain a smile and Luke's eyes widened in disbelief.

"That'll teach you to get fresh with the contest winner," Jordan said between laughs. "I guess she showed you."

"It was an accident," Eugenia insisted, looking absolutely horrified. "Really, it was an accident."

Suddenly Luke lifted his head and roared with laughter. "Dammit, Jordan, you must have hit Eugenia's hand. You'd do anything to make me look a fool and be right about destiny, wouldn't you?"

"Oh, but he didn't," Eugenia protested. "When you put your arm around me—" Her words trailed off and she looked helplessly at Lindsey, hoping her sister would rescue her.

Lindsey giggled. "When he put his arm around you, your pulse raced and your insides trembled. Your hand was shaking so badly that you lost your grip on your glass. It that what happened?"

"Lindsey!" Eugenia cried. "A lot of help you are!"

Luke put his arm back around Eugenia's waist, oblivious to both the photographer shooting away and a waiter hurrying to clean up the spilled wine.

"Well, since that was the case, I'll forgive you," he drawled with a wink. "When Cupid shoots his arrow, no one can foresee the damage he'll do, can they?"

Eugenia was about to sputter some response, but she couldn't think of a thing as the photographer thanked them, chuckled to himself and left.

"Oh, good heavens," Eugenia cried. "This is awful! I can't even begin to imagine what pictures that man might use."

Luke gave her a little squeeze, and Eugenia tried to ignore the shiver that raced over her. "Not to worry, my dear Watson. He's on our side. Anyway, I get final approval on the shots, along with the station and the hotel."

Breathing an audible sigh of relief, Eugenia tried her best to settle down. "I *am* sorry about the wine," she murmured, noticing that once again Lindsey and Jordan were lost in conversation.

Luke reached over and kissed her on the cheek. "I can't think of anyone else I'd want to ruin a shirt for me."

"Is it *ruined*?" Eugenia asked, mortified again. "Please let me pay to replace it."

Luke chuckled. "I wouldn't dream of it. I'm not even going to try to get it dry-cleaned. I'm going to save it as a souvenir." Suddenly he winked slyly at her. "No, I have a better idea! I'm going to send it to Jordan as a Christmas present."

"You wouldn't!" she whispered.

He grinned broadly. "We do these things all the time. We're forever trying to best each other, all in good fun. He's really something when you get to know him."

Smiling, Eugenia nodded in agreement. "I believe you. I've never seen anything like the magic spell he's woven around Lindsey. If you knew her better, you'd understand that she doesn't usually consider men like Jordan her type."

Luke chuckled. "I told you Jordan was the real ladies' man, didn't I? Women see what's beneath the surface and they want him. He's had more marriage proposals than a rich widow."

They both laughed, but Eugenia was suddenly worried for Lindsey. What if her poor sister fell for the man? Jordan didn't sound like the marrying kind, either. It was bad enough that Lindsey couldn't catch a rich man; if she decided she wanted Jordan and couldn't have him, she really might resort to the pastries.

Eugenia looked up in surprise when Luke interrupted her thoughts by trying to get Lindsey and Jordan's attention. "Hello! Hello across the table. Does anyone want to discuss the Fun Frolic, or are you two having your own over there?"

Both of them laughed heartily, causing Eugenia and Luke to exchange a look. Eugenia envied her sister her relaxed ways with men. Lindsey was behaving with Jordan as though she'd known him a lifetime. Eugenia, on the other hand, was trembling and shaking. And yes, her pulse was racing. Maybe she *had* spilt the wine on Luke because she was a nervous wreck near him.

"We are indeed having our own frolic," Jordan announced, "but we can take a break for business. We have all night."

Lindsey giggled as though he'd said something fantastic. Eugenia gave her sister a surprised look. When Lindsey raised her brows and almost indiscernibly patted her heart with her hand, Eugenia couldn't believe it. Was Lindsey implying that Jordan had won her heart already? Oh, heavens, what an evening this was turning into!

Fortunately, the frolic did become the topic of conversation, and even that produced peals of laughter as Luke outlined the activities planned for each evening. Each night there were to be prizes for a variety of contests, including everything from best costume to best dancer. It did sound like a wonderful party, and the more they discussed it, the more grateful Eugenia was that Lindsey had entered her name and she'd won.

She wondered if she would still be able to say that when the fantasy was over, and Luke Newton stepped out of her life as swiftly and unexpectedly as he'd entered it.

# Chapter Nine

By the time the foursome had finished dinner and the frolic discussions, it was getting late. In all the merriment, no one had noticed the passage of time. Luke suddenly glanced down at his watch.

"Oops! I've got to run," he said. He'd told the babysitter he'd be back by eleven; he had barely half an hour left.

He glanced at Lindsey and Jordan, who had been like two peas in a pod all evening. Luke couldn't remember when he'd seen a couple hit it off more quickly, and he'd seen Jordan woo women before. He smiled to himself. He believed his old friend had met his match in Eugenia's dynamic sister.

"You don't have to leave yet, do you?" Jordan asked in disbelief. "Talk about a party pooper, Luke! Damn, man, I swear you're getting old! Even if you do have to get up early, you can miss a few hours of sleep once in a while."

Glancing at Eugenia, Luke smiled. "Listen to the voice of experience. Jordan Weaver, night owl, and all of thirty-one himself."

They all laughed, but inside Eugenia felt her heart sinking for the third time that night. She wondered if that was an ominous sign, like a drowning person going down for the final time.

What was Luke's rush? Had he decided he didn't like her? Oh, Lord, she realized suddenly, she and Luke had changed places! She wanted to spend more and more time with him, and he wanted to spend less and less with her.

"May I take you home?" Luke asked, rousing her from her thoughts. "Or do you want to stay here with those two and listen to them talk about how much they have in common?" He smiled and nodded in Lindsey and Jordan's direction.

"Jealousy, jealousy," Lindsey and Jordan said in harmony, then howled with laughter.

Shocked, Eugenia realized that this time she really was jealous. She didn't know what had gone wrong, but she wished she and Luke were the ones talking about what they had in common. Oh, not that she begrudged Lindsey and Jordan their happiness—she was thrilled that they were getting along so well—however, she felt empty inside, as though she had lost some part of herself.

She couldn't explain it. Luke had certainly never been hers to lose. She hadn't even wanted him! Still, she took hope from the fact that there was still the party in which she and he would have to be involved. She shook her head. What on earth was she thinking? Now she was glad the man *had* to spend time with her.

"Yes," she said, forcing a smile. "I'll ride home with you, if it isn't too much out of your way."

"Not at all," Luke said, tempted to tell her that he wished they didn't have to leave so early.

However, he wasn't ready to get into the whole situation of Joyce and the girls. Tonight he wanted to think only of Eugenia for a few minutes. He had ached to kiss her again all through dinner. He fully intended to do at least that when he walked her to the door.

They said their good-nights to Lindsey and Jordan, who were busy trying to top each other with parting comments. No one was surprised when Lindsey called out cheerily, "Don't wait up for me, Genia. You old folks get your rest. Jordan and I may be late—like midnight, or some such ungodly hour."

The couple laughed again, as though Lindsey had said something really funny. Luke and Eugenia smiled at each other. Lindsey and Jordan's laughter was infectious, no matter how silly the conversation.

When they were in the car, Luke said, "I have to apologize again. This just hasn't been my night. I was late and have to leave early. I hope you don't mind."

"No," she assured him. She was just pleased he'd asked to drive her home. She was afraid he was going to vanish again, and she would be left wondering when she'd hear from him.

After they had parked in the driveway of the beach house, Luke got out and opened Eugenia's door. Disappointed again, she had hoped he would linger awhile in the car and talk with her. Her heart was pounding as he helped her out, then tucked her arm beneath his.

"We need to pick out our costumes," he said. "Do you have some free time tomorrow—say about two in the afternoon?"

She nodded, relieved that he'd planned something definite. "Yes, that will be fine." She laughed lightly. "I have lots of free time."

They stopped at the front door and Luke suddenly tilted her chin. "I wish I had more time to spend with you tonight, Eugenia, but I promise I'll make it up to you at the party." Then he bent his head and softly caressed her mouth.

Eugenia wound her arms around his neck eagerly, hungrily. She knew now that this was what she had been praying for all night. She wanted Luke's touch; she wanted to feel his hard body against hers. She wanted him to kiss her until she was dizzy, and that wouldn't take much. She was already losing herself to his persuasive mouth, his demanding, searching fingers, the masculine feel of him against her.

Luke groaned softly as he claimed Eugenia's willing mouth more passionately. He needed her tonight, and he'd been so afraid she would rebuff him at the door. His hands moved over her back, savoring the feel of her slender curves beneath the silky material of her jumpsuit. It seemed so natural, so right to mold her body to his, to know that they fitted so well together.

Eugenia met the fire and need in his kiss, her tongue twining with his. She had never known it could be like this, that love could be so exciting, so fulfilling.

Love! The word shocked her, but she was too lost in Luke's embrace to really explore it. Instinctively she felt this was where she belonged, in Luke's arms, lost in this moment in time, somewhere beyond the reach of reality and everyday life.

When he kissed her throat, she arched her neck, relishing the feel of his lips on her skin. Eugenia felt breathless, and flushed when Luke's lips continued down her throat to the V exposing a hint of the soft swell of her breasts.

Luke stroked the silken skin with his tongue for a moment, sending shivers over Eugenia. Suddenly he shuddered and pulled away.

"My God, woman," he said thickly, "I've got to get home before I forget what I'm even doing here with you tonight." He drew in a steadying breath. "I'll see you tomorrow at two. Good night."

Then he turned and strode down the driveway to his car.

Her pulse racing, her heart pounding, Eugenia tried to recover enough from Luke's sensual assault to make herself go into the house. Her legs didn't seem to want to work. She was shaking inside. She was a total wreck. And Luke was driving away!

Somehow she entered the house and reached her bedroom before she fell completely apart. She lay down, fully clothed, and tried to sort it all out in her mind.

What was happening to her? Was she in love with Luke? And what about him? Did he care? Why had he rushed away in the middle of their loving? She certainly wouldn't have broken it off so abruptly. Was he sorry he'd kissed her?

She didn't know whether to laugh or cry. She was terribly confused. Her mind was spinning and her body was burning. What did it all mean? And what would she ultimately win in the contest of a lifetime? Would it be a fantasy come true? Or was there only heartache in store for the queen after the party ended?

Eugenia was awakened the next morning by the sound of someone repeatedly rapping on her door. She felt as though she was in a fog; she knew she had slept badly, but wasn't even sure why. During the night she had awakened, too uncomfortable to rest well, but too sleepy to determine what to do about it.

"Come in," she half moaned, knowing it could be no one but Lindsey at the door.

"Good heavens! Look at you!" Lindsey cried.

Eugenia had no idea what her sister was talking about. Did she look that bad, for heaven's sake? She glanced down at herself, and was shocked to find that she'd slept in her expensive new jumpsuit. In fact, she still had her shoes on!

"My word," she groaned. "No wonder I slept so poorly."

"No wonder indeed!" Lindsey exclaimed. "And there I was on the other side of the door, dying to know how your evening ended with Luke. Well, I don't think I'll ask."

Eugenia smiled at the memory of Luke kissing her. She chose to dismiss her turmoil and confusion afterward, and dwelt only on that tantalizing time in his arms.

"Actually, it was fine," she said.

"Meaning?" Lindsey asked, clearly confused. "You certainly didn't get into something more comfortable— not even to sleep."

"Lindsey!" Eugenia cried. "Of course I didn't get into something more comfortable. I was perfectly fine in my jumpsuit."

"Obviously," Lindsey drawled. "It must be more comfortable than it looks, for you to sleep in it."

"Oh, Lin," Eugenia muttered, brushing at her hair. She did feel like an utter fool. Never in her entire life had she gone to bed fully clothed. "How did your evening end?"

Lindsey smiled sweetly. "Much better than yours, apparently. Jordan and I went dancing. We didn't get back here until well after midnight." Her brown eyes glowed. "And then he kissed me! *Several* times, in fact."

The dark-haired woman rolled her eyes. "His kisses are hot enough to steam up any car window." She laughed. "That's what he told me kids in the fifties did—sat in the car at drive-in theaters and smooched."

Eugenia smiled, but kept silent about her own steamy kisses. "Well, I'm glad you had a good time, Lin." She searched her younger sister's face. "Need I tell you that you've rapidly become—what word shall I use—infatuated with Jordan Weaver?"

Lindsey laughed. "That's probably as good a word as any—for now." She turned away. "Well, I just wanted to see if you were still alive in here. I've got to get dressed for work."

She looked back over her shoulder. "Genia, I'm sorry things aren't working out better with you and Luke. To tell the truth, I really did hope you'd like each other." She shrugged before Eugenia could say anything. "Maybe something magical will happen at the fifties party. They say the fifties were an innocent time, a time of dreams and romance, a time of love and marriage and planning for the future."

Eugenia watched as her sister closed the bedroom door. If anything more magical happened, she didn't think she could bear it. Luke had already brought more magic into her life than she could handle. If the party really was all that it was planned to be, she would at least have those memories.

Oh, but how empty her life would seem when Luke was no longer part of it. She didn't know how he had become so important to her in such a short span of time. She just knew she couldn't deny that he had.

When Luke arrived at two o'clock, Eugenia was waiting. She hoped he couldn't see the eagerness, the excitement in her eyes.

"Hi, Luke," she said warmly when she answered the door.

Luke smiled at her. Her blue eyes were glowing and she seemed as excited as a child. He sensed that somewhere along the way she had dropped her barriers. He wasn't quite sure when or why, but it was clear that she was no longer shutting him out. Still, he wasn't about to hurry love with this woman, no matter how badly he wanted her.

"Hi, Eugenia." He stepped inside and drew her into his arms. "Great balls of fire, you look gorgeous in that red color," he told her, his gaze roving over the shorts and blouse she wore.

She smiled. "A fifties song title, Watson?"

He laughed. "Only part of one, if memory serves me, and you really do look lovely."

She shrugged, a little embarrassed. "I thought I should wear something simple for trying on clothes."

"Simply flattering," he whispered, one hand sliding around her waist to draw her to himself. "I've told you before that you have beautiful legs," he said thickly as he lowered his head to touch her lips. His kiss was brief and tantalizing, and Eugenia's heart began to pound immediately.

She slid her arms around his neck and pressed herself closer to him, unashamedly wanting to feel his body against hers. He was the most tempting man she'd ever met in her life, and she'd lost all her defenses against his

charms. At that moment it never occurred to her to think
about other women in his life. She wanted Luke Newton
for herself. She'd known it for days now. She couldn't
resist him.

His tongue dipped between her lips to trace her teeth
and the inside of her mouth, causing her to shiver. Luke
let his lips cling to hers for a long moment, then stepped
back.

"Are you ready to go? We're going to have the store all
to ourselves for one hour, and I told the owner we'd be
there at two-thirty."

Hardly able to concentrate on what he was saying,
Eugenia nodded mutely. The only thing she was really
ready for now was more of Luke's loving. He stirred her
as no other man ever had—as she was sure no other man
ever could.

And yes, she knew how dangerous that could be, but
it was too late now. The time for caution was past.

He clasped her trembling hand and led her to his car.
After he had helped her inside, he went around to the
driver's side and stood there breathing deeply for a moment, trying to gain control of his runaway emotions.
Lord help him, he believed he was in love with the
woman!

She had been so warm and willing in his arms that he
was convinced she cared for him, too. But what now? She
really didn't know about his life, about his children. And
he had meant to take things so much more slowly.

At the very least, he had to get through the Fifties
Frolic with some kind of decorum: for Eugenia, for
himself, for the station and for the hotel. It simply
wouldn't do for the disc jockey to be seen fawning all
over the contest winner, no matter how suggestive his

comments had seemed on the radio. That was all part of the party plan.

His words had been meant to interest the audience, to add to the excitement, to build anticipation. When the audience attended the party of a lifetime, Luke had to show them as much attention as he showed Eugenia. That would be a trick, if he'd ever had to perform one. All he could think of was this woman, day and night, night and day. She was in his mind constantly.

That simply wouldn't do! Real life couldn't enter into the fantasy fifties party. The station's owners would fire him if they knew how far out of bounds he'd stepped with this woman already. Sure, he was expected to take her out on the town and talk to her about the party; sure, he was expected to fire up her enthusiasm, to flatter and make her comfortable with himself.

He was not, however, expected to seduce her. That would create a bad name for the hotel, for the station, and for future contests. He didn't know when or how something that had started out as ego, challenge, rejection or heaven only knows what had come to this point. His behavior was hardly professional.

The irony was that one of the reasons the station had set up his persona as a ladies' man was because they knew he really wasn't one. Jordan had wanted to host the contests, but the station had quickly ruled him out, because he was a ladies' man who would have to spend time separately with the winner.

Luke smiled. They didn't trust Jordan. They would pull their hair out by the roots if they knew what had been on his own mind from the first time he touched Eugenia Latrop. He put a stick of gum into his mouth and got into the car.

"Gum?" he offered, holding up the pack to Eugenia.

She honestly didn't think her hands were steady enough to grasp a stick, although she wanted one. "No, thank you," she said. Every time she looked at Luke, she felt as though she were gawking at him like a star-struck teenager. She tried to concentrate on the lyrics of a fifties song when Luke turned on the ignition; the radio was tuned to his station, for a change.

"We're getting the audience ready for the Fifties Frolic," he said, smiling at her. "I really do love this music. The time was so much more romantic, the lyrics so basic, so upbeat."

He began to sing along with the song and Eugenia smiled at him. "Lindsey sings with the songs on the radio," she said.

Luke chuckled. "Sometimes I still think you'd like to give me to Lindsey if you could figure out how, but I hate to tell you that I think it's way too late for all of us. Lindsey and Jordan definitely look like a couple to me."

*And are you and I a couple?* Eugenia desperately wanted to ask, as she pretended to listen to the song. A woman was singing about wanting her man to be her baby tonight.

"They used 'baby' a lot in the lyrics in those days," Luke commented, causing Eugenia to look at him. "I think it's a sweet endearment, don't you?"

She smiled at him. "Yes, I really do. When I hear a man say it, it makes me think the woman is pampered and cared for, protected. Somehow loved in a very delicate, gentle way, as though she were a precious and rare treasure." She smiled. "Like the care and love one lavishes on a baby, I suppose."

Luke looked back at the road. He wanted to tell her how much he wanted to pamper her, to protect her, how much he cared for her. The more he was with her, the more qualities he saw in her that he wanted in a woman: sensitivity, concern, vulnerability, the capacity to love.

He really believed that a person had to be vulnerable to love and be loved; otherwise, the outside shell became too hard to penetrate, the soul too elusive. One had to take the bad times that inevitably came in life and still believe that good triumphed.

To him, love itself was the way Eugenia had described the term "baby": love had to be pampered and nurtured; it had to be treated delicately and gently, like the precious and rare treasure it was.

When he fell in love again—hell, he didn't think he'd ever been in love before! He knew for sure that he'd never felt like this. He had a sudden desire to ask Eugenia if she'd be his baby tonight, if she'd be his baby for all the nights to come in their lives.

Eugenia glanced at him when he didn't answer, and she thought her heart would stop beating. She shouldn't have rattled on so. She felt ridiculous.

"I sounded silly, didn't I?" she murmured. "Going on about the endearment."

Luke smiled gently at her. "No, you sounded wonderful. I feel the same way you do. I like to call a woman 'baby.'"

He wanted to call her "baby." He wanted to ask her how many other men had done so before him. He realized he was jealous. The realization always surprised him. He'd never considered himself a jealous person before Eugenia came into his life.

Eugenia wondered how many women Luke had called "baby"—too many, she was sure, and suddenly she fell silent. He had reminded her too blatantly that there were other women in his life. There was no way she could avoid remembering now.

Luke's hazel eyes searched her face for a moment, then he, too, fell silent as they drove to the shop. Abruptly he turned into a parking lot.

"We're here," he said, glancing down at his watch. "And right on time."

Eugenia managed a smile; she was determined not to let her worries about the future ruin this experience. She really was excited that she and Luke would have the vintage store to themselves for an hour to select anything they wanted for the party. The fifties clothing had been set aside for them, and at least in Eugenia's case, she was allowed to keep whatever she chose today.

When Luke rapped on the door, the shop owner, a beaming man in his sixties, came to answer.

"Come in. Come in," he said. "I heard you mention my store on the radio yesterday, Luke, and you wouldn't believe the business I got! They're coming in for the fifties look for the party, so I'm glad we agreed on today for you two. I want to put the stock back in the main room when you're finished." He winked. "Good business, this idea!"

Luke laughed as the happy man closed and locked the door. "We're just as pleased as you are, James." His hand at Eugenia's back, he moved her forward a little. "This, of course, is our contest winner, Eugenia Latrop. We really appreciate you letting us select from your stock, especially from your collection of movie stars' clothes."

James grinned again. "My pleasure. My pleasure. Believe me, I know it's going to be worth it to be connected with this party."

He rubbed his chubby fingers together, indicating the money he anticipated. "Anyway," he added, "I want someone to enjoy what I've devoted my life to. They're not just someone's discards to me. I search them out by decade. I know you and the young lady will enjoy the clothes at the party."

"You bet!" Luke said enthusiastically. "It's really going to be fun. By the way, you are coming, aren't you? You know we're planning to introduce you and thank you for donating the outfits."

"I wouldn't miss it!" James said emphatically. "I'm really looking forward to it. I've already gotten tickets for my two granddaughters."

"James, you didn't need to do that. You're to get in free, as well as any guests you want to bring," Luke said. "I thought you understood that."

James grinned. "I did, and I will go free, but I got the girls tickets because they wanted to be independent." He shrugged. "You know teenagers."

Luke smiled. "I'd be happy to reimburse you."

"Nonsense. Come on back and pick out your clothes. I want to see what this pretty woman likes from the fifties."

Eugenia blushed a little. She wasn't sure herself what she would want. She'd never been much of a shopper, but she couldn't wait to see the articles now.

When James had taken them to the back room and shown them the selection and dressing rooms, he left to catch up on his book work. Eugenia and Luke didn't know which way to turn. There were racks of fifties garments, men's clothes on one side and women's on the other.

"Look, Luke!" Eugenia said, spying a full plaid cotton skirt and a huge crinoline hanging on the same rack.

Luke laughed. "You would want that, instead of one of those pencil-slim skirts to show off those pretty curves of yours, wouldn't you?"

She smiled and tried not to let him see how flattered she was by the compliment. "I told you I'm old-fashioned."

"And I admit I believe it," he said, his smile faint. "Why don't we start in the order of the party—pick out the bathing suits first, then the teenybopper clothes for the second night, then the formal wear for the third night?"

"Okay," she said. She smiled when she realized she'd succumbed to his habit of saying okay, and it didn't even bother her.

"I want to see you in the swimsuit," he murmured.

Eugenia shook her head. "No way. I'm saving all my selections for a surprise for the party."

"Don't be cruel," he teased. "Just let me see the swimsuit and the formal."

"Aha! Another fifties song title," she said.

"You've found me out, Watson," he joked. "Now tell me you won't be cruel."

"I'll do no such thing! A woman of mystery is supposed to be much more exciting to a man."

Luke couldn't imagine this woman being any more exciting than she was already. "You're going to pick out that plaid skirt with the crinoline," he said. "So already I know a third of what you'll wear."

"You're not sure of any such thing," she insisted, although she was positive the skirt would be the one she chose. "It's a secret, and that's that!"

"I'll bet you were a lot of fun as a teenager," Luke said, wondering if it was true and really trying to find out more about this woman. "You probably turned every boy's head in school."

She shook her head. "Wrong, my dear Watson. I was the bookworm; Lindsey was the party girl. She just had that magic, that excitement about her from the day she was born. I think it's in the genes, or it isn't.''

''Were you jealous of her?'' he asked solemnly.

Eugenia laughed. ''Not at all. I adored her, right along with everyone else from the day she was born. She made my life so much fun. She still does. She's crazy.''

''Do you want children, Eugenia?'' Luke asked, startling her from her thoughts of Lindsey. He couldn't imagine her not wanting them, but it was possible. He'd known more than one teacher who said he or she had had enough contact with children all day to cure them of ever becoming parents.

She smiled, as if he had asked a very foolish question. ''Of course. I just told you I'm old-fashioned.''

''How many?''

''More than a man like you could possibly believe, Luke Newton,'' she answered quickly, the knowledge painful to her.

''Oh?'' he murmured.

''Yes. It's not fashionable these days when 1.2 children are considered the norm, but I want four: two girls and two boys.''

''Why not go for six?'' he asked, wanting very much to tell her about Jeanie and Betsy.

''No way,'' she insisted. ''Four's my limit, and I have a feeling you're making fun of me, at that. Six really would be too many, because I want to keep teaching. It wouldn't be fair to anyone.''

Luke seemed pensive as he digested the information.

Eugenia laughed. ''I don't even know why we're talking about children, for heaven's sake. I'm not about to have any until I'm married, and you're not about to have any—period!''

She looked at him, knowing that she very badly wanted him to refute the statement, to say something, she wasn't even sure what.

Luke's hazel eyes searched her face for a moment. She had been emphatic about the number of children she wanted. Four. Not six.

"We'd better make our selections before James has to reopen the store to the general public," he said, turning away from her.

Eugenia watched him go to the men's side and start searching through the racks. All of a sudden she'd lost most of her enthusiasm for shopping. She had that empty feeling inside again. Somehow she didn't think it would ever be filled up. The thought hurt deeply in a way she found indescribable.

But she knew enough to sense that it had to do with her heart.

## Chapter Ten

The Friday morning of the first day of the frolic, Luke picked up Eugenia in a chauffeured, 1957 white Cadillac to take her to the resort hotel where she would stay for the three days of the party, and where she would have her beauty make-over and photo session. Luke had persuaded the station to let Lindsey room with Eugenia at the hotel, which wasn't out of line, anyway, since a married woman would have been allowed to bring her husband.

Luke, too, was staying at the hotel, because of all the time he would have to spend there making sure things were running smoothly, and because it was one of the benefits of being the hosting disc jockey. Their costumes for the fifties had already been sent to the hotel and everything was progressing on schedule, albeit with the usual confusion involved in dealing with such a massive crowd and major occasion at a brand-new hotel with completely new employees.

"How are you?" Luke asked when Eugenia had set-tled in the back of the car with him. "Are you excited?"

"I really am, Luke," she confessed. "And nervous, too!"

He squeezed her hand. "You'll do fine. I promise."

He just wondered how he would do. He couldn't even sit by this woman without wanting to confess that he'd fallen in love with her. Thank God, she was going to be in Myrtle Beach for another week before she returned to Lynchburg. He didn't know yet how he was going to make her his, but he knew she wasn't getting away from him.

When Eugenia met his hazel eyes, she believed him. She was terribly nervous, but Luke would be there at her side, helping her, supporting her, easing her along as his cohost. She knew he would let Lindsey do the things Eugenia was most worried about. Lindsey wasn't ner-vous at all!

"Can I see you after your make-over?" he asked.

Eugenia shook her head. "I want that to be a sur-prise, too."

"Why is it, woman, that you want me to have all these surprises this weekend?" he asked, only half teasing. "I don't know if my poor heart can take it."

Or mine, she wanted to say. She was in love with Luke Newton, of that she had no doubt. Still, she couldn't be sure about him, despite his interest and ardor. He had kept his distance since the day they'd selected the clothes, only talking with her once by phone. The uncertainty ate at her. Was she only his for the weekend? Or was there a chance for more?

She was lost in her thoughts when the car stopped in front of the most magnificent hotel she'd ever seen in her life. Luke had refused to bring her out to see it, even though the announcement of its grand opening and the party had been all over the news. He'd wanted this to be her surprise, and it was!

"How absolutely magnificent, Luke," she murmured.

"Isn't it?" he agreed. "It's almost like a self-contained city. It has every convenience possible, and it's right on the beach. Now, tell me," he murmured, "are you sorry you agreed to be my cohost?"

"No, Luke," she said honestly. She hadn't been sorry for days. In fact, she'd only been ecstatic. Ecstatic and nervous. Happy and worried. Eager and concerned.

"Well, let's go see what the queen's suite looks like," he said, grinning at her bright eyes and trembling smile. "You look like you can barely contain yourself."

She giggled. "I can't. I swear, I'm as bad as Lindsey. I'm so excited, I don't know what to do. I wish Lindsey could be here with me now."

"No," Luke said. "This has to be your big moment, your grand entrance. You know the photographers are waiting. They're going to make a big to-do about all the 'before and after' stuff."

Laughing nervously, she said, "Let's hope they can make the 'after' look better than the 'before.'"

Lightly he brushed her cheek with his lips. "I doubt that they can do much to make a pretty woman prettier, but they can try."

"Oh, I didn't mean that, Luke," she protested. "I meant—"

He shushed her with another kiss on the lips. "Let's go," he said, motioning for the chauffeur to open the door.

In moments Eugenia was whisked into the hotel, cameras snapping as she went. It was silly, but she felt like a queen already, and the party hadn't even started. Just being by Luke's side made her feel important.

The manager himself took her up to her suite. Luke lingered just inside the door, watching with a pleased smile on his face as Eugenia gasped while she went from room to room. Three of them had a view of the city or the ocean, each beautiful, each filled with gardenias, which were so fragrant that they almost took her breath away.

Suddenly Eugenia spun around and raced back into Luke's arms. "Luke, it's wonderful!" she cried.

He held her for a moment, wishing more than anything that he could kiss her, that he could lay her down on the big bed and make her his, that he could—

The manager smiled at them and started out the door. Luke gently disengaged Eugenia's arms from his neck. "I love an appreciative winner," he drawled, "but let's thank Mr. Martin, the manager, too."

A blush rising on her cheeks, Eugenia clasped her hands in front of her and managed a meek smile for Mr. Martin. "Thank you so much. It's more lovely than I could have ever envisioned."

He winked. "You know the entire staff is at your disposal, Miss Latrop. You have only to summon to have us do your bidding."

She grinned. "This really is a fantasy, isn't it?"

"We hope to make your stay most memorable," he said. "Just let me know if I can be of service."

She nodded. "Thank you."

"And I'll see you at six-thirty tonight," Luke said. "The cookout begins then. I'll have time afterward to explain what's expected of you as cohost. I'll come here for you."

Eugenia wanted to ask him to stay a little longer, but nodded again and watched as he left with the manager.

Wishing Lindsey would hurry up and join her, Eugenia sat down on the bed and looked around at the beauty surrounding her. It had all seemed so much grander when Luke was here.

By six that evening, Eugenia was dressed in a black, one-piece swimsuit from the fifties. It was strapless, with a simple band across the top of the bosom and just the hint of a skirt over the tops of her thighs. On her it was perfection, and even she knew it. It really was as though she belonged to another time, to a simpler life-style than the eighties.

But it wasn't really the swimsuit that astonished her by its ability to flatter her. She had, indeed, been transformed by her beauty make-over. Her blond hair had been highlighted until it looked like spun gold, yet it looked as natural as if she'd been born with it.

The stylist had shortened it, permed it in soft waves, and had given Eugenia bangs. Her brows had been slightly darkened, and her blue eyes seemed bigger and bluer than ever.

"You look absolutely smashing!" Lindsey said. "Real cool, man! Far out! And whatever else they said in the fifties. Lord, I didn't know it was possible!"

"Well, thanks a lot," Eugenia said with a playful hint of sarcasm in her voice. "You sound like I looked like the witch of the North before all this was done."

Lindsey giggled. "You know I didn't mean that. Would I say that about a sister who at least bears some resemblance to me? It's just that you look so lovely now, Eugenia. I mean it. You really are beautiful. *I* want a beauty make-over, no matter how much it costs."

Eugenia laughed. "*You* don't need one. My word, girl, just look at you!"

Lindsey's curves were even more voluptuous in the fifties swimsuit she'd chosen. It was a one-piece suit, too, in a navy color, but there wasn't a hint of a skirt to it—and the strap around her neck only served to call attention to her generous proportions.

"Thanks, Sis," Lindsey said, "but truly, I have to confess that you outdo me by far tonight." She walked over and hugged her taller sister. "I'm glad you won, and I'm glad you agreed to take part. I honestly think we're going to have the dream party of a lifetime."

Eugenia's eyes were moist. "I do, too, Lindsey. I really do."

They both jumped when someone knocked on the door. "That's Jordan," Lindsey said. "He can't wait! I told him not to come until six-thirty with Luke, but—well, you know—I think the man's in love! He can't stay way from me!"

"And you, Lindsey?" Eugenia asked earnestly. "How do you feel about him?"

Lindsey shrugged carelessly, as though the question were totally unnecessary. "I love him, too, of course."

Eugenia gasped. "Is that true, Lin? Why you hardly know the man! What happened to Brad?"

Lindsey held up her hand. "Brad who? Girl Scout's honor. I don't even remember Brad. I know I love Jordan."

When another rap sounded, more loudly this time, Lindsey hurried to the door to answer. Sure enough, Jordan was standing there, a big grin on his face.

"Don't keep your man waiting, woman!" he demanded playfully, suddenly picking Lindsey up and whirling her in the air. "Gosh, do you ever look beautiful! I might even propose to you, if you keep looking so good to me."

Both of them laughed. "See you downstairs, Genia," Lindsey said, grabbing a beach cover-up and sandals as she rushed out the door with Jordan.

Eugenia could only marvel at the couple. She realized for the first time that she hadn't heard Lindsey go on about marriage since she met Jordan. Well, no wonder; he was the one talking about it. That was quite a change for Lindsey, a welcome one, Eugenia was sure.

Left alone for thirty minutes, she found herself wishing Luke had come to claim her early. There was nothing to do but pace the lovely rooms and gaze out at the ocean with its assortment of swimmers and boaters. She smiled at the thought. Never had she felt more beautiful, more like a queen, never had she known such luxury and excitement. All that was missing from the fantasy was Luke.

She felt breathless when he finally knocked at her door. "Eugenia, it's Luke," he said in that sexy voice. For a moment she was sure she felt her heart flutter like a Victorian maiden's supposedly did. She was sure she was a little dizzy. Would Luke like the new and revised fifties-style Eugenia?

With a trembling hand, she opened the door. The sight of Luke standing there in a black, boxer bathing suit really took her breath away. He had on a white shirt that was rolled up at the sleeves and buttoned partway, but there was no way to avoid seeing the thick, curling hair on his chest.

Eugenia tried her best to stop staring, but when she realized that Luke was staring at her just as intently, she broke into laughter. "Have we met before, mister?" she teased.

She was surprised by the huskiness of his voice. "I've never met a woman as beautiful as you, lady, I'm sure," he said.

She made a little curtsy. "Thank you, kind sir, and won't you come in?"

Still staring at her, he shook his head. "I dare not, as tempting as you are. Anyway, it wouldn't be proper for me to be in such a beautiful lady's room, would it?"

Eugenia didn't let on that she was disappointed. She wanted Luke to say more about her new look; she wanted him to come inside and kiss her. She wanted that and oh, so much more.

"I'll just be a minute," she said. "I'll get a beach wrap."

"That seems such a shame," Luke murmured, not moving from his spot outside the door. "You look ravishing, Eugenia. Honest-to-God ravishing."

She felt her heart flutter again as she pulled on a black-and white-striped terry wraparound garment that completely covered the suit.

"It's a real crime to cover all that loveliness," he murmured, secretly grateful that she had. He ached with wanting her.

"I'm ready," she said, hanging a shoulder bag over her arm.

Luke was ready, too—to go into her bedroom and make love to her. Fortunately, they had an entire beach full of guests, who had been so eager that they had arrived early.

"We've got our work cut out for us," he said. "The band is going to start playing any minute now, and I have to take the first hot dog. We already have fifty or sixty people out on the beach. I think maybe some of them have been there all afternoon."

"It sounds like the party's going to be a great success," Eugenia said, a little shiver racing over her at the thought of all those people.

Luke laughed. "You bet. Jordan and Lindsey are already down there, stirring up the crowd."

"I can believe that," Eugenia said with a smile. Her pulse racing, she stepped into her shoes and went with Luke to the elevator.

When they arrived on the beach, a cheer went up from the crowd. She saw that it had been instigated by Jordan and Lindsey, but it caused her heart to pound, anyway. She had never imagined such a fanfare in her life. She and Luke were the waited-for parties, and the music started playing when they walked out onto the huge, wooden balcony that led to the beach.

Cooks in white uniforms, aprons and fifties-style caps were at their stations all around the balcony, cooking hot dogs. Mr. Martin, the hotel manager, went to the microphone where the band was situated and introduced Eugenia and Luke. Then Luke turned the first hot dog and handed it on a plate to Eugenia. Jonsey, the photographer, was there to capture the moment.

From then on, the party was in full swing, and Eugenia thought she'd gone to heaven. She had never had so much fun in her entire life. She, Luke, Lindsey and Jordan judged dance contests, gave away prizes for everything from the most authentic costume to the most outrageous one, and through it all, she felt as if she belonged in the spotlight by Luke's side.

She was still laughing when Luke led her away at midnight, saying she would turn into Cinderella if she didn't leave the ball. She and Luke went to the microphone to bid the others good-night, for many of the approximately five hundred were still there, having the time of their lives.

"We *were* a success," Eugenia whispered to Luke, when they were in the elevator and on their way to her suite.

"Did you really ever doubt it?" he asked.

Eugenia was reminded that this was the old Luke she had first heard on the radio, but now she smiled. "I doubted I could pull it off," she confessed, "but, no, I never doubted that you could."

"Well, thanks for the vote of confidence, lady," he said, drawing her near. "I never doubted that you could. Didn't I tell you from the first night that this would be good for you?"

"And it has been, Luke," she said seriously. "It's all been like a dream. Thank you so much for all but demanding that I accept as winner. I'll never forget this weekend."

"I hope not," he murmured, dipping his head so that he could kiss her parted lips.

Eugenia knew that this was the most beautiful part of a lovely evening. She'd missed Luke's kisses. All too soon, the elevator stopped, and Luke drew away from her.

He held the button when the door opened. "Good night, Cinderella," he murmured. "Sleep well."

More disappointed than she wanted to let on, Eugenia whispered, "Good night," then stepped out of the elevator. She knew Luke watched her until she'd opened her door, but when she looked back over her shoulder, the elevator doors were closing. She had only a glimpse of Luke before he was gone.

Sighing, she tried not to let the final moments of the night dampen all the joy she'd known. But deep inside she was terrified that all the nights would end like this, especially the third one. Would Luke then leave her life forever?

Eugenia never knew what time Lindsey came to her room. She awakened to the sound of someone knocking on the door. Her first thought was of Luke, until she heard Lindsey opening the door, and then she smelled coffee.

Tumbling out of bed, she went into the living room and stared at her sister as Lindsey sat down before the elegantly set table that room service had delivered. There was a pot of coffee on it and an assortment of pastries.

"I don't believe this, when we can go to the dining room and have *anything* we want!" Eugenia cried, laughter spilling from her lips.

"Hey!" Lindsey retorted. "It doesn't get any better than this for breakfast, no matter where you go! Come on. Eat! Enjoy! Feast! Be merry!"

Eugenia sighed as she sat down and poured herself a cup of coffee. "Wasn't last night divine?" she murmured dreamily. "I never imagined it could be like that."

Laughing happily, Lindsey shook a finger at her sister. "See! I told you so, and you didn't even want to do it. See what you would have missed out on? And if I'm any judge of things, you and Luke seem to be getting along just fine, too. Or is that only for the public?"

The mere question caused Eugenia's heart to sink. Was it only for the public? Somehow she'd forgotten that she was just a contest winner. Intentionally or unintentionally, Luke had convinced her that she was so much more. Suddenly she was afraid to let Lindsey know how involved she was with Luke Newton, how much she cared. She didn't want to be his fool as she had been Daniel's.

She shrugged. "I think we like each other well enough now."

Lindsey giggled. "That's an improvement over the initial meeting, isn't it?"

Both women smiled, then began to talk about the coming night's planned activities. Eugenia had indeed selected the plaid skirt with the crinoline, a wide belt and a white blouse with a Peter Pan collar. Lindsey, of course, had chosen a pencil-slim skirt and a lightweight sweater to accentuate her sexy figure.

Eugenia had a photograph session set up for mid-morning. She would have been frantic if Lindsey hadn't agreed to go with her. For the occasion, Eugenia was provided with clothing, which she was constantly being hustled into and out of. Actually, once she relaxed with the photographer, she did so well that it was decided she and Lindsey would both be used as the models on the literature to promote the new hotel.

When they had finished, they ate a light snack before dressing for the second night of the party. Neither Eugenia nor Lindsey had heard from Luke or Jordan all day, and both were obviously eager to get down to the ballroom, where the teenybopper night was being held. It sounded like even more fun than the beach party had been.

Both sisters laughed when they saw each other dressed in their fifties costumes. Eugenia's crinoline caused her skirt to flare out around her body, making her belted waist look even smaller than usual. She wore bobby socks and saddle shoes, and had a ribbon in her hair.

"Man, are you the most!" Lindsey cried. "I think that's what they said in the fifties. Or was it 'real cool, cat'?"

Eugenia laughed. "Whatever it was, I get the idea, and the same to you, Sister."

Lindsey did look just as cute in her fifties outfit, although much sexier, of course. But then, Eugenia thought with a resigned sigh, Lindsey looked sexy no matter what she wore.

"I wonder what Luke and Jordan will wear?" Lindsey asked.

"I don't know," Eugenia said, "but I'm eager to find out. Let's go."

"You're on, Sister," Lindsey said, as they hurried from the room in search of the two disc jockeys.

## Chapter Eleven

When the sisters saw Luke and Jordan on the stage in the ballroom, which was empty—the crowd was waiting outside the locked doors—they went to join them. Both men were dressed in rolled-up dungarees and white T-shirts. Eugenia and Lindsey kept laughing as they were introduced to an authentic band from the fifties, their dress similar to the deejays' outfits.

They tried their best to concentrate as they were told more about the program for the night. The winners of the bunny hop and stroll dance contests were to be given a free weekend stay at the hotel. There were all kinds of prizes of varying importance.

Eugenia and Lindsey sat down in folding chairs while Luke and Jordan talked with the band. Soon it was time to let in the revelers. Luke took Eugenia's hand and led her down to open the doors. Suddenly Eugenia looked down at the floor as they walked.

"Oh, my goodness!" she cried, her eyes wide as she glanced at Luke. All around her, little flakes were falling onto her socks, shoes and the floor. "What is it?"

Luke seemed equally surprised. Then he reached down and lifted her skirt a little.

"Luke!" she protested. "What are you doing?"

He chuckled softly. "I think your slip has dandruff, honey."

Chagrined, Eugenia lifted her skirt higher. The crinoline was so old and had been unused for so long that the starch had cracked when Eugenia sat down. It was crumbling right before her eyes.

"Oh, no!" she moaned. "What will I do?"

"Very elementary, my dear Watson," Luke said, tugging at the layers of fancy white material. "We discard this particular item."

"I guess there's no other choice," Eugenia conceded, feeling utterly foolish as she held onto Luke's shoulders, while she hastily stepped out of the slip.

"What'll I do with it?" she murmured, hoping the band and Jordan and Lindsey had been too engrossed in conversation to notice what she and Luke were doing.

His eyes glowed wickedly. "This, my sweet, is going to be Jordan's birthday present, flakes and all!"

"Luke, you wouldn't—"

But she knew he would as he quickly stuffed the cumbersome crinoline under the nearest table, which had a lacy scarf around it and was laden with food.

"I hope no one peeks under there," he muttered behind his hand.

Eugenia looked down at her suddenly deflated skirt. "Luke, doesn't this look awful now?"

He grinned and shook his head. "I like it better. I know where you are now under there. But we must hurry.

The doors should be opened. We don't want the natives to get restless.''

Giggling, Eugenia opened one door while Luke opened the other, then both of them stepped aside and gazed in amazement at what the crowd considered fifties teeny-bopper clothing. Everything imaginable was there in glorious colors and strange combinations, from leather jackets to beehive hairdos. One girl even came complete with a hula hoop draped across her chest, as though it were an an accessory.

She won the best-dressed contest, but the bunny hop winner was Lindsey, unanimously chosen by the other three judges, Eugenia, Luke and Jordan, as well as the entire band, one of whose members had to get out and show the party-goers, including Lindsey, how the dance had really been done back in the fifties. Graciously—and cleverly, as it turned out—Lindsey offered her prize to the second-place contestant. Jordan was very pleased, and later offered her a special prize, just from himself.

Teenybopper night turned out to be even more fun than the previous evening. The dances mainly involved groups, and the entire crowd seemed to loosen up and get friendlier with each other. The band members mingled freely with the people, teaching dance steps and commenting on clothing.

Everyone seemed thrilled with the event. No one wanted it to end at midnight, but Luke once again insisted that his cohost and guest of honor would indeed turn into Cinderella if she didn't retire.

Eugenia, minus her crinoline, was as reluctant to leave as all the others. The band agreed to play one more slow song, by way of contrast to the many fast ones they had played during the evening. Eugenia smiled, anticipating Luke holding her close, but to her surprise, he whisked her away while the lights were dimmed and everyone was still dancing.

In the elevator, she was unable to contain her disappointment. "Luke, I wanted to dance the final song, too," she complained.

Luke broke into hearty laughter. "Some help you are, cohost. You're *supposed* to be helping disperse the crowd on a nice note, leaving them with good memories of a spectacular night."

"Oh, it was spectacular," she conceded. "That's why *I* hated to leave."

Grinning, Luke said, "What a party girl you turned into! Dancing the night away! Laughing and playing with the audience! Insisting that your pick win the stroll contest—a dance which I'm sure you've never even seen. If the band hadn't howled in protest, why, you'd probably have given the prize to that woman."

She laughed. "I have turned into a party girl, haven't I? And I have seen the stroll done on old TV reruns." Her blue eyes met his. "Luke, you were so right about this whole thing. I have more confidence at this moment than I've had in my entire life. Honestly, I think it'll make a difference forever in the way I relate to other people, to my students, to their parents, to my peers. I know you won't believe this, but I still get stage fright when someone unfamiliar sits in on my class. I think that's all behind me now. I mean, how much more of a crowd can watch than five hundred people?"

"Isn't that the truth?" Luke pulled her to his side and hugged her. "You feel so much better without that dreadful crinoline," he murmured. "It's no wonder those things went out of style."

She giggled. "I hope it's still under the table where you stashed it."

"So do I. Won't Jordan get a surprise when he receives *that* in the mail?"

They both laughed, but the laughter died on Eugenia's lips when the elevator stopped; once again, Luke ushered her out with only a brief kiss. She wanted to complain about that, too, but didn't want to spoil what had surely been the two most wonderful days of her life.

"I'll see you tomorrow night at six," Luke said. He winked at her. "By the way, I heard the news about you and Lindsey being made the official models for the hotel brochures. The first thing I know, my lady will forget all about teaching and become a big-time fashion model."

Eugenia laughed. "In fifties clothes? I doubt it. Anyway," she said seriously, "a teacher is all I've ever wanted to be. I would never give it up. Lindsey might be another story."

"And a mother?" Luke said.

"Lindsey a mother?" Eugenia shook her head. "Somehow I don't think so, but stranger things have happened."

"No," he said softly. "I meant you. All you've ever wanted to be was a teacher and a mother. Four children, I believe it was."

She nodded and smiled faintly. Luke sounded oddly melancholy, as though he were disappointed in her. It made her suddenly feel sad. She had changed, it was true, but she obviously wouldn't ever be the kind of woman Luke wanted.

A teacher and a mother. Yes, that was what her destiny was all about. She'd known all along that wouldn't appeal to a man like Luke, but hadn't allowed herself to dwell on it once she fell in love with him.

She slipped out of the elevator without even saying good-night; she didn't even wait for the sound of the elevator doors closing. When she had dashed into her room, she went to the window and looked out at the beach. Suddenly the fading summer night seemed very cold and lonely. Not even the nearly full moon warmed the picture before her. Eugenia closed the blinds and went to bed.

The third and final night of the three-day party was at hand. Eugenia had never looked lovelier, and she knew it. She was dressed in a pale blue, strapless gown of double-layered chiffon with a draped, fitted bodice and skirt that hugged her body until it suddenly flared out in a long, full train at her hips. Floor-length and worn with brocade ballet slippers, the confection was the most gorgeous gown she had ever seen. Actually it was timeless in its beauty, and was made for someone just like herself.

She really felt like a princess, a queen, or someone equally lovely and regal. The hair stylist had swept up her hair in waves off her face and shoulders, with a light scattering of bangs across her forehead, which accented her eyes. Gone were the familiar glasses, and in their place were new contacts. Eugenia hadn't even known one could get contacts so quickly, but then, for a fantasy party apparently anything was possible.

"My God! Is that you, Eugenia?" Lindsey cried when she rushed into the room, clad in a long, tight, black gown, elbow-length gloves and a black hat with a veil. "You look incredible! I feel like a black widow spider next to your fragile beauty. Why, Princess Grace never looked so good! I swear it!"

Eugenia smiled at her younger sister. "Oh, thank you, Lin. I feel beautiful. I really do. For the first time in my life, I really *feel* beautiful."

"Luke will flip!" Lindsey exclaimed. "He hasn't seen the gown, has he?"

Eugenia shook her head. She was nervous about that. The photographer had gone on and on about how lovely she was in the gown, and, strangely and amusingly, as Luke had predicted, the man had suggested that Eugenia, with her height and coloring, would make a marvelous model. She wouldn't even consider it, of course; however, she'd been flattered and thrilled.

"Jordan won't exactly throw you out the window when he sees you, Lin," Eugenia said. "You look very sexy in all that black."

Lindsey chuckled. "Good. That's me. Sexy Lindsey! I looked for the most provocative thing I could find."

"You succeeded," Eugenia agreed.

The sisters began to talk about some of the people who'd bought tickets to tonight's affair, which was by far the most expensive evening, with a sit-down dinner and a band that was still playing in night spots all over the country.

"I'm so excited, I could split a seam," Lindsey declared.

"Oh, I hope not!" Eugenia said in mock horror. "You might bust out all over."

Lindsey looked down at her generous cleavage and both women laughed.

"I didn't mean there," Eugenia said. "You've left little enough exposed, as it is."

Lindsey pretended to try to wiggle down into her gown, then shrugged. "Well, you should talk. You look rather provocative yourself, and your skin looks so creamy and smooth next to the pale blue. You truly do look like a movie star or someone famous, Genia. I'm impressed."

"Thanks, Lin."

The loud knock on the door caused both women to jump. "Damn that Jordan!" Lindsey cried. "Does he have to do that every night? Can't he knock like someone civilized?"

Eugenia laughed. "You wouldn't want him if he did, Lin, and you know it."

Lindsey laughed lightly as she went to the door; both sisters knew Eugenia was telling the truth. When Lindsey opened the door, she stepped back in surprise. Jordan and Luke were waiting, and they looked extraordinarily handsome in their fifties attire.

Luke was dressed in black slacks, a white dinner jacket and a thin black tie. Jordan was in a blue tuxedo.

Luke threw up his hands in dismay. "My word! I've been outdone by everyone! I feel like the poor relation." He included all three of the others in the assessment, although he had eyes only for Eugenia. "You're a dream."

She couldn't look away from him. She'd been dying to know what he would say about her gown. It was really only his opinion that mattered. The other compliments had been nice, but it was Luke whom Eugenia had been waiting to hear from.

When Jordan and Lindsey said they'd see the other couple downstairs, neither Luke nor Eugenia acknowledged their departure.

"I have a couple of small gifts for you," Luke murmured. "May I come in?"

"Of course," she said. She had waited for him to ask that question for two days.

He stepped inside and opened a small, velvet box. "I think this will look lovely with your gown," he murmured as he removed a simple gold locket on a chain.

Eugenia was relieved when he put it around her neck and fastened the clasp. She was trembling so much that she was sure she could never do it. Then Luke took another box from his coat pocket and pulled out a delicate wrist corsage with a single, small gardenia.

"Thank you, Luke," she whispered, moved by his thoughtful gestures.

She wanted to laugh and joke and ask him if he did this for all the contest winners, but if he did, she didn't want to hear about it. She sensed that this was going to be the most splendid night of her life; she didn't want even a negative thought to spoil it.

"Are you ready?" he asked, when he had put the corsage on her wrist.

Eugenia wanted him to look at her, to kiss her so much, but his fingers lingered on her wrist, lightly massaging it as though he couldn't look away from the gardenia.

Breathless, she nodded. For what seemed like forever, they stayed there in that spot. Finally she drew away and picked up a stole that had been made to go with the gown.

She shivered when Luke draped it around her shoulders, and never quite knew how she found herself seated at his side a few minutes later at one of the long tables in the huge dining room. In the ballroom beyond, the band had already started to play easy-listening music. Eugenia told herself that she could die and go to heaven at this very moment without ever having missed a thing on earth. She felt beautiful. Luke was by her side. And the moment was pure glory.

Seven courses of the meal were served, but Eugenia was unaware of the passing of time or of the chatter around her. She participated, making light conversation, glancing at Luke, noting the way he made everyone feel special, but she was too wrapped up in her own cocoon of happiness to find anything to object to.

When dinner was over and nearly everyone adjourned to the ballroom, Luke suddenly drew Eugenia into his arms and eased her outside onto the massive, wooden balcony beneath the full moon. A light wind was blowing, and her gown fluttered slightly in the breeze as Luke turned her to the music.

"Eugenia, you're the most beautiful creature here tonight," he murmured against her ear. "I didn't want to share you with anyone else any longer. You don't mind being my baby tonight, do you?"

A smile trembled on her lips. "I thought you'd never ask," she whispered. "I thought you'd been avoiding me."

"I've had to," he confessed. "For the sake of the party and for my own sanity. There are so many things I want to say to you, so many things we need to discuss, but I couldn't cause a scandal by seducing you during the party of a lifetime."

She laughed nervously, like a young girl. She'd wanted him to seduce her; heaven only knew how much. "I thought you didn't like me and were only enduring the three days," she said.

"You didn't, and I know it," he murmured low.

She shook her head. "I didn't truly, but I have wondered if I have your attention only for the duration of the contest, or if you've only been trying to win me over to prove that you could, or—"

"None of the above," he murmured fiercely as the strains of the music filtered through the closed door.

Suddenly the door opened and a woman stepped forward. She had two little girls with her, holding each by the hand. Had someone else found their hideaway?

In the golden moonlight and the soft, shadowy light that filtered through the elegant draperies at the ballroom windows, Eugenia could see clearly enough to tell that it was the woman she'd seen Luke with that first night at Lincoln's Club. The little girls were the same ones she'd seen on the beach a few times. The woman was their mother.

"Luke, we have to talk. It can't wait!" the woman said dramatically.

Luke drew in a steadying breath. "Joyce, I don't believe you're doing this. Nothing is so important that it can't wait three more hours until this night is over, I'm sure."

She held up the two little girls' hands. "They are. Your daughters are more important, Luke Newton, than three hours of dancing with her." She indicated Eugenia.

Thoroughly shocked, it took Eugenia a moment to understand just what had been said. Luke's daughters? Luke's wife? At first she couldn't seem to grasp it. Then she couldn't believe it. Pulling herself free of Luke's arms, she fled, brushing past the woman and children and racing across the ballroom, as though she really was Cinderella and midnight was coming.

Or had it already? The party was over for her as surely as if the clock had struck. Luke Newton was married? How could it be? How could the station play him up as a ladies' man?

She didn't understand, but what she felt was the swift and stabbing shaft of pain that went through her heart at the thought. This was like Daniel all over again. She should never have trusted Luke. She'd known that from the start.

When she reached her room, she ripped off the lovely gown and tossed it onto the floor without a care for its beauty or for how she'd felt wearing it. The party really was over.

Tears stung her eyes as she shed her underclothing and headed toward the shower. She wanted to wash away everything connected with Luke Newton. She wished it were possible to get inside her mind and scrub it free of him, too.

Suddenly someone literally beat on the door. Eugenia didn't want to know who it was. She kept walking toward the shower.

"Eugenia, open the door," Luke called out.

Eugenia ignored him.

"Eugenia, don't make me beg," he called louder. "Don't leave me standing out here in the hall, humiliating myself by begging you," he demanded harshly. "You don't even know what's going on. I can explain. Don't keep that door closed against me."

The word "humiliation" penetrated, whether Eugenia wanted it to or not. She knew it all too well. She hesitated only a moment before pulling on a robe and answering the door.

"Get it over with, Luke," she said bitterly. "I don't want any drawn-out explanations, and I believe you have not two, but *three special gals* waiting for you."

"You'll not get any drawn-out explanations," he replied bluntly. "I've tried to tell you about my special gals—my two little girls—several times, Eugenia," Luke said simply. "I've tried to tell you that I'm not the ladies' man the station made me out to be."

"If I can count, I believe there were *three* females downstairs with you, weren't there?" Eugenia said, her voice catching. "In fact, I've seen them all three at the beach near Lindsey's house. And, correct me if I'm wrong, wasn't that your *wife* in Lincoln's Club with you that night I went to meet you?''

"Yes, to the first question," he agreed. "They live near Lindsey. And they're still downstairs. No, to the second question. I'm happy to be able to correct you and say that the woman is my ex-wife."

"Ex-wife?" Eugenia murmured, wanting so desperately to believe him. If it was only true, then nothing else mattered. Nothing! She loved this man so very much!

"Yes, ex-wife—for a number of years now." He managed a half smile. "That's what's so amusing about me being a ladies' man. My best role is that of father, and that's the truth. I love my daughters, and I wasn't about to engage in a romance lightly a second time."

He shook his head at the irony. "The radio station knew that. With my two special gals and an ex-wife, they realized I'd be perfectly safe behind the radio persona of ladies' man. It was Jordan they were worried about—Jordan, single and the biggest flirt in town."

Eugenia looked into his eyes and knew that Luke was telling the truth. She felt as though she'd behaved like a fool by running away again, without giving him a chance to explain.

"I've been hurt before, Luke," she murmured.

He smiled gently. "I surmised as much, because so have I. The woman downstairs almost cured me of love—almost," he murmured.

"My fianceé had other women while we were engaged," Eugenia said, realizing that it didn't matter at all anymore. Luke and the word "ex-wife" were what mattered, and the fact that Luke was nothing at all like Daniel.

"That's all in the past," Luke said. "The future is what counts. My ex-wife wants to remarry, and she wants me to share custody of the children with her. I asked you twice, Eugenia, if you'd like six children. I'm asking you again. Please don't say no. How about four girls and two boys? We can handle them, I promise you."

"We?" she barely whispered.

"We. You and me. I love you so much it hurts, Eugenia. But I love my little girls, too. I want us to be a family."

He loved her! Eugenia's heart sang at those precious words. "Oh, Luke—" she breathed.

"And you don't have to worry about giving up teaching," he continued quickly, afraid she would counter with some reason why his dream couldn't come true. "I was a communications teacher before Joyce found that position too boring for her social life. I gave it up in the name of love and became Luke Newton, disc jockey. Now I want to go back into teaching. I've got résumés out around Lynchburg, and it's looking good for me."

Eugenia smiled, almost unable to believe what he was telling her. Luke—a teacher? Luke wanting her to be part of his family?

"I want to marry a teacher named Eugenia and have four more children," he hurried on, as though frantic to get it all said, before she could tell him she wouldn't agree. His voice was such a contrast at the moment to that of the smooth, suave Luke Newton on the radio. "Please don't say no, Eugenia. I'm really very good with children. You'll see. Six will be a piece of cake. Say you'll marry me."

Still smiling, Eugenia rushed into his arms. "Oh, Luke. I love you! I want to marry you. Yes! Yes! Of course, I'll marry you. I adore your daughters already. We can have ten children if you want! Four was just a number—a number until I met you. We can live anywhere—work anywhere—just as long as you love me."

Luke hugged her tight. "Oh, sweet, sweet Eugenia, you literally have no idea how much I love you. I thought such happiness would never be mine, but you've just made me the happiest man alive."

When he slid his hands inside the robe, he groaned deeply. "Oh, Lord, you don't have a stitch on under that garment." His gaze burned as he looked at her. "You are beautiful. Absolutely beautiful, woman."

Suddenly the door literally burst open. "Eugenia! Eugenia, Jordan and I are getting married!" Lindsey squealed, dragging in Jordan behind her. "That was my special prize!"

Shaken by all that had happened, Eugenia took a steadying breath and looked from Luke to Lindsey and Jordan, both of whom were all aglow and clearly in love.

Eugenia wondered if she and Luke looked that way. "We're getting married, too," she blurted, still unable to believe her own joy, much less Lindsey's.

"You are?" Lindsey asked, seeming to come out of a fog. "How wonderful, Eugenia! And Luke," she said, nodding at him. She giggled. "I almost can't believe all this. How about a double wedding?"

"I—er—I—" For the first time ever, Jordan seemed at a loss for words. "I think we can wait a little while to discuss that, Lindsey," he said. He looked pointedly at Eugenia's robe, seeing that Eugenia had pulled it together and that Luke was trying to tie the sash. "I think we're interrupting something."

Eugenia's face flamed when she realized what Jordan was implying. "Oh, no!" she cried. "I was changing clothes when Luke came to the door. I—"

Luke kissed her briefly to shush her. "You were interrupting, Jordan," he said with a broad grin. "Congratulations to you and Lindsey. Now if you don't mind, I was still in the process of proposing."

Jordan and Lindsey laughed loudly, then left as Eugenia's face grew redder.

Luke didn't even wait for the door to close before he drew Eugenia into his arms again. "I think you just agreed to marry me," he murmured.

"I think I most certainly did," she whispered.

Luke's mouth found hers, and claimed it with all the passion and desire he'd held in check for three long days. Three fantasy days that would last forever.

*   *   *   *   *

*Silhouette Romance®*

# LONG, TALL TEXANS

## Diana Palmer brings you the second Award of Excellence title

### SUTTON'S WAY

In Diana Palmer's bestselling Long, Tall Texans trilogy, you had a mesmerizing glimpse of Quinn Sutton—a mean, lean Wyoming wildcat of a man, with a disposition to match.

Now, in September, Quinn's back with a story of his own. Set in the Wyoming wilderness, he learns a few things about women from snowbound beauty Amanda Callaway—and a lot more about love.

He's a Texan at heart . . . who soon has a Wyoming wedding in mind!

The Award of Excellence is given to one specially selected title per month. Spend September discovering *Sutton's Way* #670 . . . only in Silhouette Romance.

RS670-1R

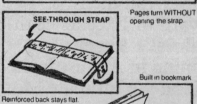

**NORA ROBERTS**
brings you the first
Award of Excellence title
**Gabriel's Angel**
coming in August from
Silhouette Intimate Moments

*They were on a collision course with love....*

*Laura Malone was alone, scared—and pregnant. She was running
for the sake of her child. Gabriel Bradley had his own problems.
He had neither the need nor the inclination to get involved in
someone else's.*

*But Laura was like no other woman...and she needed him. Soon
Gabe was willing to risk all for the heaven of her arms.*

The Award of Excellence is given to one specially selected title per
month. Look for the second Award of Excellence title, coming out in
September from Silhouette Romance—**SUTTON'S WAY**
**by Diana Palmer**

Im 300-1